A NIGHT IN
BABYLON

A NOVEL

MICHAEL WEST

Published and Distributed by:
Foundations 4 Readiness
Los Angeles, California
Foundations4readiness@gmail.com

Packaging/Consulting
Professional Publishing House
1425 W. Manchester Ave. Ste. B
Los Angeles, California 90047
323-750-3592
Email:.professionalpublishinghouse@yahoo.com
www.Professionalpublishinghouse.com

Cover design: TWA Solutions
First printing March 2020
978-1-7346922-0-4
10987654321

For inquiries contact: foundations4readiness@gmail.com.

Dedicated to everyone fighting the good fight.

CHAPTER ONE

Enemy Lines

"Suspect is heading east on Slauson! Requesting back up immediately!"

Lightning split the firmament as Officer Cooper made a sharp turn at a dark and deserted intersection. He was yelling over the radio with his foot pressed hard against the gas pedal, and the siren was blaring as heavy currents of rain flooded the windshield. His partner, Officer Higgins, appeared rather exuberant while firing his Beretta out the passenger-side window.

"This guy's fucking crazy!" he hollered in the wind.

Speeding with a clenched jaw, Cooper was focused on the bright taillights blazing recklessly ahead. The storm was only getting worse, and nights like these made early retirement more appealing. The chase began in Ladera Heights, after receiving an anonymous tip regarding a man who was not only armed and extremely dangerous, but also connected to a known terrorist group called the Stay Ready Soldiers; and anything related to the SRS, the protocol was always shoot to kill.

"I repeat, suspect is heading east on Slauson! We need back up, damn it!"

Finally, a mechanical voice sounded from the console. "Back up is en route," it said apathetically.

After half a dozen misfires, Higgins was forced to reach inside the glove compartment for another magazine. Drenched from the rain, his heart was racing uncontrollably, and his hands were shaking from the adrenaline as he reloaded with wide eyes. As a rookie, he hoped his ambition would compensate for his lack of experience.

"I can't get a clear shot," he complained. "I think he has run-flat tires…"

"Maybe you can't shoot," Cooper told him.

"Maybe you can't drive," Higgins countered, aiming outside once again.

The grizzled Cooper was hunched forward with both hands gripping the steering wheel, chasing the elusive vehicle through a desert of shadows and concrete. Weary of killing, the seasoned lawman had seen more than his share of bloodshed. He initially joined the force to make a positive difference in his community, though he was now at war with the very people he swore to protect. Riding the storm, he made some impressive maneuvers to close the gap, before his partner opened fire once again. Freckling the speeding car with bullet holes, Higgins unleashed a flurry of ammunition, determined to end the pursuit once and for all.

Suddenly, the suspect hydroplaned across another intersection, and Cooper was shocked to see a young woman in the passenger seat. She was beyond beautiful, with features that were both dark and alluring, like a rare flower from antiquity. The attraction was more than a mystical seduction, and he became enchanted as time and space stood still, allowing her eyes to pierce the very depths of his true nature. In less than a nanosecond, he concluded that she had to be a hostage, tangled in an endless web of psychopaths with guns and vendettas. He figured this was his chance for redemption, to finally do something good; to be the hero and save the damsel in distress. Distracted by his own valiant thoughts of gallantry, he never noticed the AR-19 in her hands.

"Cooper, look out!"

BRAT-TAT-TAT-TAT!

The tides swiftly turned as a downpour of rounds exploded through the windshield, gruesomely killing Higgins in a hot shower of bullets and broken glass. Before Cooper could react, his torso was mutilated by the flurry of scorching metal, and thick waves of blood washed over the dashboard. He collapsed with his face planted in the steering wheel, and the vehicle swerved wildly until it somersaulted off the road, resulting in a fiery crash.

As the flames illuminated the night, the enchanting woman sternly reclined with her weapon on her lap. She was a certified warrior, with incomparable skills and invaluable courage. Her name was Kali, and she was more dangerous than she was beautiful.

"I'm out of ammo," she voiced, her hair soaking wet.

In the driver's seat, a young man with the demeanor of a seasoned veteran was focused on the dark void ahead. He was steering with one hand, chewing a toothpick with fire in his eyes. Speeding through the barren streets, the road was silent and unforgiving, a blur of shapes and colors that made his mind race twice as fast.

"Geronimo, you can slow down now…"

Bolting past a flashing traffic light, he could feel surges of heat radiating from his left side. He managed to get himself shot in the chase, and the pain was inescapable. Bleeding on the leather interior, he reached inside the breast pocket of his Army jacket, and retrieved a jagged cigarillo stuffed with marijuana. Though it was damaged in the ordeal, the deformed blunt was still in smoking condition. After placing it between his lips, he began fumbling through his remaining pockets for his gold lighter.

"This just keeps getting better and better," he grumbled, unable to locate it.

Beneath the hazy glow of a looming skyline, Kali leaned against the headrest with a heavy sigh, listening to the rain as her mind drifted above the noise. Reality was hell, and death was always around the corner. The past few months had been nothing less than a living nightmare, full of close encounters with the Grim Reaper. She took a deep breath, recalling simpler times, and eventually spotted the missing lighter between her boots.

She casually picked it up, then waved it around playfully, but was immediately taken aback when Geronimo extended a bloody hand. "You're bleeding!" she blurted.

He snatched the gold lighter with a scowl on his face, then put the flame to what looked like a broken twig. As he inhaled the medicine, Kali noticed the blood soaking through his clothes, and instinctively reached over for a better assessment. However, he gently pushed her away as thick clouds of smoke poured from his nostrils.

"It's nothing," he grunted. "…This car's done; we need a new one." His words were through clenched teeth, and each breath was like a knife against his insides.

"You need a medic," she told him.

Most of the car was blanketed in bullet holes, and empty shell casings were peppered throughout the cabin. Submerged in a sea of darkness, Geronimo checked the rearview mirror to ensure they weren't being followed, then glanced subtly at the woman responsible for saving his life numerous times. He was always on the run, whether from the law or from himself, and never allowed anyone to get close to him. Nonetheless, he found solace with her.

Eventually, he parked the mangled heap beneath a deteriorated Metro station.

"We almost got assassinated back there," he said, exiting the wreck. "We're behind enemy lines…every pig in this city's out for blood."

"It was an ambush; someone had to have tipped them off," Kali thought aloud. "You think they know about Bunchy?"

"Maybe," he uttered. "…Maybe he's dead already."

The rain subsided, exposing a red moon behind a thin layer of rolling black clouds. As Geronimo led the way past a decrepit fence, Kali was staring at the blood cascading from his jacket. They were in a section of the city that had long been abandoned and forgotten by the world. Feral dogs were howling behind condemned buildings, and the cold air carried the toxic fumes of industrial waste.

After traversing the desolate backstreets, avoiding coyotes and rabid rodents, they finally entered a crumbling parking structure overgrown with wild vegetation. Broken pillars draped in colorful graffiti stretched toward the thunderous sky, and a thousand lights from downtown shimmered ominously in the distance. While navigating the maze of jagged stonework and tangled greenery, Geronimo spotted a familiar tarp camouflaged amongst the rubble. He removed the moldy wet covering, magically revealing a black luxury sedan with tinted windows. Reaching under the front bumper, he retrieved a silver key from behind the air dam, then remotely unlocked the doors.

Kali was almost impressed once she sat upon the soft leather upholstery.

"This is definitely you," she marveled, surveying the sleek interior.

Falling in the driver's seat, Geronimo took one last hit of the crooked blunt before flicking it away, then the engine roared louder than a wild animal. It started raining again, and thunder bounced off the atmosphere as they accelerated east, deeper into the urban wilderness. With one bloody hand on the wheel, Geronimo reached inside the glove box, and retracted another blunt that was perfectly symmetrical. As he sparked it aflame, Kali shook her head despite herself. She averted her eyes to the storm, fearing for the fate of their comrades.

"Better fasten your seatbelt," Geronimo told her, speeding across the wet pavement. "It's looking like one of those nights."

CHAPTER TWO

No Tomorrow

Bunchy's Pawn Shop was at the edge of Huntington Park near the Los Angeles River. The two-level complex was surrounded by the remnants of a once flourishing neighborhood, gradually fading into obscurity. A middle-aged Bunchy purchased the property after a mysterious fire many years earlier. Despite all odds, he had it refurbished and ready for business in less than eight weeks. He was a true entrepreneur at heart, with a considerable amount of money retained from his youthful days as an arms dealer. His shop was always open, and customers respected him for his vast selection of unique merchandise, as well as his uncompromisable integrity.

"Bullshit!" shouted a lanky pale-faced man. He had a mouthful of missing teeth, his beard was disheveled, and his windbreaker was completely saturated from the storm, causing a puddle to form around his soggy sandals.

Across from him, Bunchy was sitting in his favorite chair behind a glass display counter, calm and cool as usual. Smoking a cigarette, he was closely examining a fancy watch under a giant magnifying lamp.

"I'm telling you it's fake," Bunchy stated.

"You're full of shit!" the man hollered. "This here's a Presidential! It's worth like twenty-thousand!"

Bunchy reclined in his leather chair as smoke danced above his flat cap. "I hear you talking," he smiled, dangling the watch from his index finger. "Problem is…this ain't no Presidential."

Standing by the front door, a tall man wearing a black trench coat and matching dread cap was quietly reading the latest issue of *Bullets 'n Clips* magazine. His name was Samson. He was built like a refrigerator, with a solid gold medallion wrapped around the muscles that used to be his neck. Reviewing an article on armor-piercing bullets, he tried ignoring their verbal banter, though he considered their conversation exponentially annoying.

The disorderly man was turning red as he continued to shout. "What the fuck is it then?" he argued.

Bunchy tossed him the watch, and he barely caught it with both hands. "I'm sure you're familiar with replicas," Bunchy told him. "Exhibit A." He extinguished his cigarette in a bronze ashtray on the counter-top, then stood from his chair with a subtle smirk. "You know where the door is," he added, turning to walk away.

The customer grabbed him by the arm. "Let's try this again," he insisted, his eyes wide and bloodshot.

When Bunchy turned around, he was surprised to find himself at the business end of a small revolver. There was a moment of awkward silence, as if all the air left the room. Smelling like a tub of hard liquor, the scrawny man made a gesture toward the cash register.

Bunchy shook his head. "You sure you want to try that?" he questioned.

"Just give me the money," the man snarled, pulling back the hammer.

He suddenly felt the cold end of a Winchester press against the back of his head, and the daunting sound of a shotgun pump froze him perfectly in place. He turned around slightly, and from the corner of his eye, he could see inside the dismal abyss of a stainless-steel barrel. He nearly defecated at the sight.

The man behind the shotgun was Samson, and he happened to be Bunchy's first cousin, although they were more like siblings. "Don't be foolish," he growled. "If it's a tombstone you want, that can be arranged."

The customer nervously averted his gaze back to Bunchy, only to have a black Smith & Wesson pressed against his brow. "Holy shit," he whimpered.

With his head between two cannons, he closed his eyes as Bunchy lifted the small revolver from his palm, and a sudden crash of thunder almost gave him cardiac arrest. "Let me take care of this one," Samson grunted.

"Nah, be cool," said Bunchy. "This here's a place of business. And how's a man supposed to conduct business with a shotgun pointed at his head?"

"Very carefully," Samson grumbled.

Samson reluctantly took a few steps back, then angrily suppressed the Winchester beneath his trench coat. Meanwhile, the would-be thief remained motionless, too afraid to breathe. Bunchy lit another cigarette, then playfully whistled for his attention. The man slowly opened his eyes to an all too familiar grin.

"Well, that escalated rather fast," said Bunchy, tickling the trigger of his gun.

The scraggly man finally conjured up the courage to speak. "I, uh—"

"No need for apologies," Bunchy interrupted, blowing smoke in his face. "Lucky for you, I'm actually in a generous mood tonight. Maybe it's the cheerful weather outside, or maybe I don't feel like mopping up your brains from my floor. So…what's it worth to you?"

Judging by his facial expression, the customer was clearly puzzled.

"The watch, Einstein," Bunchy clarified. "How much?"

"Right, uh…twenty-thousand?"

Bunchy pulled back the hammer in disapproval.

"Did I say twenty?" the man stammered, sweating profusely. "Uh…I meant to say ten."

With a dramatic sigh, Bunchy reached inside his left pocket, then pulled out a hefty knot of money wrapped in black rubber bands. "I'll give you fifty bucks to politely get the hell out of my store."

Knowing the timepiece was worthless, the customer was too stupefied to speak.

"You're right, let's make it a hundred," said Bunchy, peeling a crispy bill from the lump in his hand. "But if we ever catch you in here again, I promise it won't be as pleasant."

Paranoid and confused, the man slowly stretched out his hand to retrieve the money.

"Careful," Samson warned him. "Don't forget about the Presidential."

After realizing he was still holding the replica, the unkempt man desperately threw it on the glass counter, then Bunchy nonchalantly released the currency. With the paper in hand, the man cautiously made his way toward the entrance, avoiding eye contact. However, before exiting the shop, he paused timidly by the doorway, and spoke without turning around. "Thanks," he said, leaving with a new perspective on life.

Samson casually approached the display counter. "So, we're a charity now?" he scoffed.

"He wasn't worth the bullet," Bunchy replied, tucking away his pistol.

Examining the revolver taken from the would-be thief, he was surprised to discover the chambers were empty. He laughed to himself as he set it aside, then picked up a remote control that was next to the overflowing ashtray. He pressed play, and an old classic rhythm began resonating from the speakers mounted on the walls, soothing his spirit with a simple melody. He sat down in his favorite chair with a sigh, then lit another cigarette with the one he was already smoking.

"He wasn't worth a hundred dollars either," Samson voiced.

Bunchy chuckled under his breath. "It's called an investment," he exhaled.

"I don't care what you call it. I'm the type to call a spade a spade, and I know what I saw…"

"And what's that?"

"You're getting old, cuzzo; you're starting to get soft."

Thunder rolled as the rain increased exponentially, and the wind began howling like a demon from the other side. At almost fifty-years old, Bunchy had accumulated enough wins and losses to last him a lifetime. He left home at an early age, and after learning all the hard lessons, he was an assembly of experiences that separated him from the rest of the world.

"Maybe," he shrugged, refusing to argue. "I don't know… maybe I'm just tired."

Michael West

"Shit, welcome to the club," sighed Samson.

Rummaging through a rotating magazine rack, he was pleased to find an iconic copy of *Wet 'n Nasty*, a popular adult publication that recently went bankrupt. After picking up the explicit material, he returned to his preferred location by the door.

"I remember when that would've ended differently, though," he added, slowly flipping through the pages. "Like when I had to stop you from pistol-whipping Ricky over a poker game."

"That was a lifetime ago," Bunchy countered.

"That was last week."

"Last week?"

"And don't forget about Sandra's party," Samson continued.

"Here we go..."

"You shot at her husband."

"Who knew that fool was her husband?"

"I'm just saying, you're the only one I know that's banned from Hollywood Park."

"Lies, all lies," Bunchy insisted.

"If you say so."

Suddenly, the electricity went out, and everything fell into a deep state of darkness. Unable to see, Samson tripped over a small stand of alligator boots, and stumbled against a shelf of power tools.

"Damn it!" he blurted.

Bunchy started laughing when he heard the clatter. "See that?" he chuckled. "Keep talking shit."

"Will you shut the hell up and help me? I think I broke something..."

"Hold up, I'll get a flashlight. I think the fuse box is down in the—"

KABOOM!

Without warning, a massive explosion obliterated the entire front entrance. The detonation lifted Samson completely off his feet, catapulting him across the room into a rack of vintage video games. Bunchy was knocked from his chair, and his back slammed against the wall as a deluge of fiery debris surged throughout the room. Slumped in the smoke, his ears were ringing, and his vision was hazy, but he had to recover quickly, because a dozen federal agents in tactical gear were raiding his shop. He had just enough time to duck behind the giant display counter as bullets spiraled in his direction. Staying below the line of fire, he cursed aloud and covered his head as shards of glass shattered from above, causing blood to trickle down from his ear.

As the lawmen swarmed his property, Samson was playing possum on the floor, and managed to grab one of them by the boots. Pulling him to the ground, the two began wrestling for supremacy, but Samson easily had the upper hand. He quickly disarmed the agent in the tussle and, with his knee planted atop the man's sternum, discharged his Winchester at point blank range, violently ending the contest. However, more agents were emerging from the smoke. He pointed his shotgun at his attackers, then emptied a cluster of rounds without hesitation. After striking two in the torso, he rolled behind an antique, dropleaf table, dodging a string of bullets.

"Bunchy!" he yelled over the gunfire.

On the other side of the room, Bunchy was crouched against the display counter with his pistol gripped tight. Staring at the shards of glass on the floor, each fragment acted as a miniature mirror, and he could see the reflection of an agent flanking his position. He swiftly turned around and fired his Smith & Wesson at the perfect time with the utmost accuracy. After laying the agent flat on his back, he instinctively picked up the extra firepower while calculating his next move. Without a second thought, he leaped from behind the counter with his finger on the trigger. Sliding across the floor, he eliminated five men at once, then continued shooting as he scrambled to a nearby custodial closet. He desperately opened the door and used it as cover against incoming gunfire.

Samson was behind a concert speaker, locked in a storm of bullets, firing round after round at an endless wave of invaders. With his adrenaline at a boiling point, he darted toward his cousin at the opposite end of the shop, dicing through a sea of agents with his shotgun pumping. He dropped down to his knees as bullets whisked past his ears, and he glided behind a row of giant flat-screen televisions. With extra shells in his pocket, he quickly reloaded as three agents blitzed his position. He lunged backward onto the floor with his gun blazing, and hollered as he canceled each of his attackers in an orchestra of explosive metal. He quickly scrambled to his feet, then continued navigating through a blizzard of shrapnel, ignoring the blood excreting from his shoulder.

Unfortunately, Bunchy was almost out of ammunition. Bullet holes splinted the closet door, and he only had a few seconds to make a move. After one last burst of gunfire, he dashed for the nearest weapon, which was soaking in a puddle of blood. He seized the automatic in one motion, then vaulted himself behind a wall of guitars while squeezing the trigger. As the sparks flew and the bodies dropped, he scanned the room for any sign of his cousin.

In the disarray of gore and debris, Samson expertly carved his way through the store like a killing machine. This was hardly his first firefight. Having a steady hand and sharp reflexes, he was on a warpath paved with death, desperate to reach Bunchy. Suddenly, a surge of pain expanded throughout his body as a metal slug ripped the flesh from his calf muscle. A second bullet burrowed itself deep inside his back tissue, and he hollered in pain as he collapsed to the floor, gritting his teeth with the heart of a lion. He leaned on his shotgun like a walking stick as he struggled to his feet, but succumbed to a flurry of rapid fire.

As Samson fell in a pool of his own blood, Bunchy saw the horror from across the room, and his reality was instantly decimated. There was a paradigm shift, and his entire world unraveled as he raced toward him without hesitation. He was operating on autopilot, firing in all directions, focused solely on the only friend he ever had.

In an explosive array of death-defying stunts, he miraculously reached Samson's side unscathed and tried dragging him behind a row of portable generators. Unfortunately, Samson was larger than a linebacker and twice as heavy. Pulling with all his might, a bullet struck Bunchy in the leg, going straight through, and he toppled next to his kin with blood gushing from the wound, immobilized by the excruciating pain. As the onslaught progressed, he was out of ammunition, trapped in a hail of bullets, disabled in the line of fire, and there was no escape from the bitter truth: Samson was already dead.

It was enough to remove all reason from logic, yet Bunchy's survival instinct was stronger than any philosophy. Thus, in a true act of despair, he protected himself by using his cousin as a human shield. Staring into his lifeless eyes, the real had become surreal, and tears poured into rivers of blood as Samson's body jolted from the mindless overkill. Sheltered from the endless torrent of bullets, Bunchy became enraged as his own guilt consumed him, and his screams of sorrow were deafened by the sound of relentless artillery. An eternity passed before the shooting stopped, and after he heard the final shell casing bounce off the floor, he helplessly waited for the bullet with his name on it. Then, he remembered Samson's shotgun.

"Better check to make sure," said an agent, reloading his assault rifle. "That one bastard killed most of our men."

"Yeah, but look at him now," said another, stepping over a dead patron in the shadows.

Bunchy could hear the enemy getting closer by the second as he carefully reached for his cousin's Winchester. Although the shotgun was only a few feet away, it might as well have been on the moon. Straining with his arm fully extended, he miraculously got his fingertips on the forend, and quietly scooped up the weapon without being seen. He gently racked the slide to ensure it was loaded, then took one last breath to ready himself, determined to give them all hell. As far as he was concerned, there was no tomorrow. Trusting his instincts, he quickly positioned the shotgun over Samson's body like a tripod, cursing loudly while vigorously squeezing the trigger.

Shooting blindly with his head low, he was numb to the world around him, waving the barrel from side to side until the shotgun was empty. Afterward, his ears were ringing as thin layers of smoke curled from the mouth of the Winchester, motionless in the silence of the dark. He was in a dire state of limbo, suspended in animation, anticipating his own demise, yet it never transpired. A moment passed before he could hear the rain pouring outside, then he cautiously raised his head to survey the room.

Everything had been destroyed in the firefight. Giant bullet holes spanned the walls, the floor was littered with piles of scorched debris and empty shell casings, and a dozen mangled bodies were scattered throughout the shop. They were all dead, and Bunchy was alone in a world torn asunder. His survival constituted the ultimate price, the bill paid in flesh.

Kneeling over a bloody corpse, he relived the horrendous scene in his mind, and wanted nothing more than to trade places with his best friend. Samson had always been there to protect him, a burden he carried even in death. The weight of it all had Bunchy spiraling further and further from reality, afflicted by his own conviction, until he was distracted by something shining in the corner. It was Samson's gold medallion, gleaming in the rubble. Bunchy was in a place outside of himself, yet he instantly became fixated on the sparkling ornament. He knew his cousin loved that necklace.

"Don't worry," he whispered in Samson's ear. "...I'll be right back."

Using all his strength, he painfully climbed to his feet. He was in a trance, dazed and confused, leaving a trail of blood as he limped through the carnage with despair in his eyes. Glistening among the shadows, the lavish jewelry had more value than any ancient treasure. It was priceless now. He somberly picked it up, then held it close, lost in his own misery, until he was abruptly shot in the back without warning. A wave of fire and electricity bolted up his spine, and he was overwhelmed with agony as his face hit the floor.

"That was impressive," said a sinister voice.

Bunchy was struggling to breathe as a dark fog clouded his senses. Straining his eyes, he could see a federal agent standing over him with a malevolent grin. The lenses in his expensive eyeglasses were cloudy, and he was wearing a bulletproof vest under his FBI raincoat. He was holding a wet umbrella in one hand, and a stainless Beretta in the other. After analyzing the shop, he casually kicked a shell from under his loafers.

"Armor-piercing bullets," he acknowledged. "Very resourceful."

He aggressively pressed his foot down against Bunchy's back, forcing him to choke on his own fluids.

"We clearly underestimated you," he admitted, pointing his gun. "I'll have to add that to my report."

Bunchy was barely conscious as he awaited his fate. He closed his eyes and accepted his destiny, comforted by the thought of being with his family in the hereafter. He had fought the good fight, he had sacrificed enough, and he was ready to die. However, before the agent could squeeze the trigger, a combat knife flew from the shadows and pierced his skull, killing him instantly. The strike was so swift, Bunchy was clueless to its occurrence. After slowly opening his eyes, he was surprised to see the federal agent on his knees, a blade lodged in his forehead.

A mysterious man shrouded in darkness yanked out the knife, and a large stream of blood sprouted high through the air.

"Bunchy!"

On the verge of losing consciousness, he recognized the voice, and a wave of relief washed over him as Kali rushed to his side. He instantly concluded that the faceless figure holding the knife could only be one man: Geronimo.

"Thank God," Bunchy uttered before passing out.

CHAPTER THREE

A Concrete Desert

Fractured buildings stretched toward a blackened sky like the frail hands of a dying man. The rain had stopped, and beneath a cherry moon were the ravished streets of a poverty-stricken metropolis. The gutters were clogged with crumbled plastic waste, and cracked sidewalks shimmered with urine and broken glass. Many of the streetlights had been shot to oblivion, and collections of bullet holes were clearly visible in various traffic signs. Abandoned monoliths had been vandalized and smeared with graffiti, and people with nowhere to go were forced to live in third-world conditions.

The City of Angels had become a cesspool of corruption, disease, poverty, and violence. Humanity was no match against the influence of their own demons. While politicians made empty promises, giant corporations profited from disparity. Amidst the unrest and dissatisfaction, riots and protests were spreading like wildfire, and anti-establishment groups were growing in popularity. The government had turned against its own people, and Los Angeles was on the verge of martial law.

Camouflaged in the night, an eight-wheeled mechanical monster was roving the vacant streets. Built stronger than a military tank, the all-terrain vehicle was large and heavily armored, equipped with powerful weapons mounted on its shell. The monstrous machine had an electromagnetic rail gun, an automatic grenade launcher, plus a GAU-19 heavy machine gun at its disposal. The carrier traveled swift and deadly, like an iron beast on the hunt, utilizing artificial intelligence for navigation, and plates of light-bending nanotechnology that made it virtually invisible.

Inside the tank, six passengers sat quietly under ultraviolet light, each fully suited in highly advanced ballistic armor made with elastic polymers. They were a team of mercenaries, an elite unit known as the Black Hawk Battalion, mostly tasked with counterterrorist actions and engaging heavily armed criminals, all in the name of fortune. Each member was exceptionally trained in urban warfare tactics and operations, making them extremely dangerous. Although their true employer was a private company known as Hydricore, they had been contracted by the CIA for a mission of the utmost importance: to eliminate the last of the SRS.

Sitting in the rear compartment was a man with hands larger than oven mitts and tattoos around his thick neck: they called him Dozer. With a next-generation combat rifle resting comfortably at his side, he was watching a prerecorded news program on a holographic tablet. Next to him, a young woman with a multicolored buzzcut and dark freckles was attaching a M26 shotgun to the barrel of her weapon: they called her Sparks.

"Shouldn't you be getting ready?" she asked. "Now's not the time for your cartoons."

Dozer proudly brandished his rifle. "I'm always ready," he boasted.

Across from Sparks sat two other killers, and both would have rather had their guns do the talking: their codenames were Maverick and Hennessy.

"He's probably watching that talent show again," Maverick snickered.

"You're missing out," Dozer countered. "Last week, some guy set himself on fire for the win."

"How's that a talent?" Sparks frowned.

"It's not; but it's damn entertaining," Dozer admitted.

On the transparent touchscreen in his hand, an orange-faced man was sitting at a sleek anchor desk in front of a computer-rendered backdrop. He was wearing a three thousand-dollar suit with an expensive hair piece, and had an eerie cosmetic smile full of pearly white teeth. He spoke with an arrogant confidence unlike any other television personality:

"Tonight, on Society Today, *police chief Andrew Bryson joins us to talk about the SRS, better known as the Stay Ready Soldiers. Are they freedom fighters, or domestic terrorists? And can they ever truly be eradicated? We have Bryson here to answer the hard questions and respond to his critics. I am your host, Rudolph Scott, and this is* Society Today."

"I can't believe you watch that shit," scoffed Hennessy, leaning back in his seat.

"Is our country on the fringe of collapse? Unemployment, crime, healthcare, education, immigration, climate-change; I've told you about the radiation in your water; I've told you about the economic collapse and false-flag operations. It's all going to hell in a handbasket, and Bryson believes the SRS are the number one threat to our society."

"Society's so full of shit," Sparks mumbled, laughing to herself.

"The SRS is a radical militarized group that claim to be against police brutality and government oppression. However, not much else is known about them. They're very much "off-grid", in the same vein as doomsday enthusiasts from over ten years ago. Some say they're the offspring of previous groups, such as the Poor Righteous Army or the LA Militia, but that's irrelevant at this point. They gained notoriety after claiming responsibility for the bombing of a police station in South Los Angeles, and their assumed leader, Tree Newman, released a statement claiming it was payback for the police shootings of unarmed civilians, which, by the way, is a topic we covered extensively a few months back, so make sure to check that out in case you missed it.

"Needless to say, the Soldiers are known for their aggression toward law enforcement officers. They've bombarded authorities with shootouts and firebombs, and the violence has only gotten worse. Chief Bryson's home was literally burned to the ground not too long ago, and he barely escaped with his life. Dozens of officers have been killed, and innocent civilians have been caught in the crossfire. Mayor Dernum even declared a state of emergency, enforcing a ten-o'clock curfew zone, and requesting assistance from the national guard. All of this reached a boiling point last week when Mr. Newman was ultimately shot and killed by police officers."

Still examining her weapon, Sparks inserted an extended magazine, then pulled back the bolt handle.

"So, got any plans this weekend?" she asked innocently.

"Not really," Dozer shrugged. "Probably watch the fireworks."

"Now, before the break, I want to remind everyone that next week is the two-year anniversary of the 'Southland Quake'. As you all know, that earthquake had the highest ground acceleration ever recorded in America. It had a magnitude of 8.8 on the Richter

scale, and it was felt further than Las Vegas. We're talking billions of dollars' worth of damages. Thousands died; even more were injured. It's one of the worst natural disasters in recent history. But was it truly a natural event, or a coordinated strike? I should save that topic for another time. Anyway, people like Ted Dernum keep draining the budget, and they have downtown looking like the Emerald City. Meanwhile, everywhere south of the 10 Freeway is still in shambles. It's time to demand more from our elected officials, more from our politicians and our leaders—"

In the front compartment, a man was calmly resting his eyes. "Can you please cut that shit off?" he requested. "Some of us are trying to sleep over here."

His name was Rico, and he was somewhat of an outcast among the team. Unlike the others, he was a median between evolution and technology, a combination of natural selection and scientific design. After being chosen for Hydricore's "Titan" program, his body had been fully augmented, complete with bionic and cybernetic implants to enhance his strength, speed, and coordination to astronomical levels. He was a living weapon, and his potential was unlimited.

Dozer looked at him from the corners of his eyes. "I didn't know you could sleep," he said.

Rico turned around in his seat, his muscles bulging through his sleeves. "I can't, that's the point."

"I don't hear anyone else complaining."

"I'm not complaining," Rico clarified. "I'm asking politely."

"Well, put some bass in your voice next time," Dozer responded. "I might hear you better."

Rico slightly raised his chin with a welcoming grin. "Next time, I won't ask," he asserted.

As the convoy powered over blocks of rubble and debris, a chiseled shooter by the name of Junior was chewing on a licorice stick. He had a thick beard and broad shoulders, and a black bandana was tied around his head. "Y'all sound like a couple of schoolgirls right now," he chimed.

Sparks chuckled to herself as she double-checked her various grenades. "I think Junior has a point," she agreed.

"I think Junior has a learning disorder," said Dozer. "Besides, this'll be a walk in the park. Ain't that right, Tin Man?"

Rico shook his head at the remark. "You think so, huh?" he scoffed. "The SRS are tightly organized and highly capable. They're considered extremely dangerous, and they shouldn't be underestimated."

"Ooh-la-la," Dozer mocked. "I read the dossier too, motherfucker. And to be honest, I wasn't that impressed. Sounds like a bunch of punk-ass kids to me."

"You always say that," Junior voiced.

"And I'm right every time."

"Yeah, if right was left," said Rico, glaring at the dark road ahead. Passing a deserted intersection, he could see the phrase "*Welcome to HELL-A*" painted in giant red letters across a deteriorating wall.

⋆⋗══●

The Great Western Forum was once a landmark in the Los Angeles area. Built in the sixties, the Romanesque arena was famous for housing championship teams and electrifying performances. It was the place to see celebrities, concerts, political events, and even religious services on occasion. However, two-thirds of the circular structure had been destroyed in the Southland Quake. The entire roof was shaped like a concave, the exterior colonnade was toppled over, and the foundation was nothing more than a crater of twisted cables and steel beams. The Forum had become a relic, another lost monument suspended in time, destined to be forgotten.

In the shadowy parking lot, two black Suburbans were stationed side by side next to a collapsed column. Palm trees were leaning in the wind as a dark gloom covered the surrounding rubble, and the late hour was accompanied by its own apparitions and phantoms. In the rear of the Suburban, with the back door open, a half-naked teenager named Dawn was bent over into the back seat, with her face down and her panties wrapped around her ankles. Behind her, a forty-year-old cop named Garrett was thrusting his hips like he had something to prove. His collared shirt was open, and he was sweating uncontrollably. "You like that?" he huffed. "I know you like that, bitch."

Dawn was completely disengaged, and silently wished for it all to end quickly. Meanwhile, Garrett appeared to be on the verge of a heart attack. After three more awkward pumps, he finally pulled out and climaxed loudly over her lower back. The girl hardly moved a muscle, and he eventually stepped back with a satisfied grin. Grabbing a can of beer from the hood of the car, he quickly guzzled the brew, then hurled the empty canister at the coliseum. He spat on the ground, then staggered over to two other men standing off to the side.

"She's all yours, Karl," he belched. "Knock yourself out."

"It's about time," Karl hissed, loosening up his belt.

Fully aroused, he marched over to Dawn and rolled her on her back. Trapped in a horrendous cycle, she helplessly covered her face as she prayed to be anywhere else. Karl dropped his trousers, then forced himself inside her without

25

any contraceptive. "Look at those titties," he drooled, sucking on her left nipple.

The off-duty officers had been running a train on the young girl, each taking turns at fulfilling their carnal desires. This was a normal routine for them. They would often cruise the slums for desperate women to exploit, offering them drugs or money in exchange for sexual acts. They would even threaten the girls with jail-time if they refused to comply. It was easy for them to take advantage, especially in this part of town.

Standing next to Garrett, a man named Crawford was staring at the pulsing lights of a distant plane over the horizon. He was smoking a joint, drinking from a bottle of cheap liquor, listening to the grunts and moans that could be heard throughout the parking lot. "Man, couldn't we have gotten a motel?" he asked. "It's fucking cold out here."

Garrett adjusted the sleeves of his leather jacket. "And waste my hard-earned money? Fuck that," he countered. "Relax, it's a ghost town out here."

Crawford surveyed the empty landscape with apprehension. "It's not the ghosts I'm worried about," he said ominously.

"I keep telling you, we're good. Tree's dead. The Soldiers are finished, and we're on top of the world. So, stop bitching and grow a pair, please."

Crawford threw a playful jab at him in response, and Garrett laughed it off as he popped opened another beer, allowing his mind to drift elsewhere. He had caviar dreams and champagne wishes, but was stuck in a dead-end job that he hated with all his heart. He thought about the house he couldn't afford, and the car worth more than his salary. His mind was afflicted, his spirit was restless, and his soul was barren.

"Next time, we should get more than one girl," said Crawford, passing the joint.

"Spoken like a married man," Garrett replied, clutching the leaf between his fingers.

Meanwhile, Karl was at the point of no return.

"Damn it, I'm 'bout to cum!" he announced. "I'm 'bout to—"

Before he could reach his climax, a swift burst of gunfire erupted from the shadows, striking him in the back of his head. His skull divided in half, and his blood splattered over Dawn's naked breasts before he collapsed lifeless on top of her. Paralyzed with fear, she was unable to scream. "What the fuck!" Crawford choked, spitting up alcohol.

Immediately, a storm of bullets diced through the air, striking him above the shoulders, and he fell to the ground, drenched in his own brain matter. In a frenzy, Garrett scrambled around the closest car as shots shattered the windows and shredded the door panels, forcing him to drop behind one of the tires. He was out of breath as he fearfully retracted a pistol from his back holster.

On the verge of a panic attack, Dawn pushed Karl's body to the wet pavement and crawled beneath the car, desperate to escape.

As the shots echoed into silence, Garrett felt a slight chill before peeking around the mutilated grille, eyes wide with terror. "I don't know who's out there, but you just killed two cops!" he shouted.

He waited for a response, but all he could hear was his own heartbeat. After an eternity, he finally decided to make a run for it. He desperately dashed toward the street, shooting frantically at the shadows, and empty shell casings scattered across the pavement as he raced for his life, breathing heavy in a cold sweat. However, before he could get far, another burst of gunfire penetrated his kneecaps, and he fumbled his weapon as he fell to the concrete, shackled to his own pain. Crippled and bleeding out, his legs were like soggy noodles as he squirmed in place, hollering in the night.

He was still yelling when three mysterious figures surfaced from the deep. They each had a looming presence that was truly menacing, however there was one that stood out from his two companions. Tall and built solid, he had a cigarette tucked behind his ear, and a combat rifle in his hands. He was wearing a brown aviator jacket, and a pair of night-vision goggles was perched high atop his brow. They called him Red, and he was the Minister of Defense for the Stay Ready Soldiers.

"You know its dangerous out here this time of night," he scowled, towering over his prey. "Don't kill me!" Garrett pleaded, crawling away in terror. "Please, I got kids!"

"Do yourself a favor and stop talking," Red suggested.

Standing at his right was a young man wearing black fatigues and a skull cap. With a snarl on his face and his arms crossed, a carbine rifle was strapped loosely over his shoulder. Everyone called him Numbers, and he was a member of the SRS Security Council.

"That doesn't look too good," he grinned, pointing at Garrett's legs. "We might have to amputate."

"That's something to consider," Red smiled.

The third individual was carrying a rather large duffle bag. He was wearing a long black coat with a matching do-rag, and a fifty-caliber pistol was tucked in a leather holster on his right thigh. His name was Horse, and he was also a member of the Security Council.

"Sick motherfucker," he growled.

"Please, I'm a cop," Garrett begged, cowering at their feet.

Numbers immediately struck him in the jaw with the end of his rifle. "Shut the fuck up!" he flared.

Garrett spat a handful of teeth as he prayed for a deity to save him.

"Check this out, cop," Red told him.

He licked his thumb before pulling the cigarette from behind his ear. As he held it in one hand, he waved his other hand above it in a dazzling manner, and with a flick of the wrist, he made the cigarette disappear. Afterward, he rubbed his palms together, extended a clenched fist for display, then slowly opened his hand to unveil the cigarette for all to see.

"Voila," he said proudly, putting it to his lips.

Dead silent, Garrett was at the threshold of impending doom, transfixed on his own mortality.

"Maybe he doesn't like magic," Numbers chuckled.

Red sparked the cancer stick aflame, scattering ashes in the breeze.

"That's too bad," he exhaled. "Maybe he'll like my next trick."

He calmly pulled a nine-millimeter handgun from beneath his jacket, and Garrett shuddered at the sight.

"This is called the grand finale," Red told him. "So, you like underaged girls, huh? Taking advantage of them? Raping them? You devilish fuck. See, I got eyes and ears everywhere, and I know all about you, officer Frank Garrett. You and your little pals cruising our side of the freeway, acting like you own shit. Not anymore; not after tonight. You're lucky I got shit to do. Normally, I like to take my time…"

Before Garrett had a chance to argue, he was shot multiple times at point-blank range, and his blood splashed over the cracks in the pavement.

"Rotten motherfucker," Horse added.

In the shadows of an urban desert, Red flicked his cigarette at the dead cop, then turned around in a huff of smoke. His comrades followed suit, and the trio returned to the gruesome scene of broken glass and brain matter. They searched the bodies and vehicles for weapons and ammunition, taking anything of value for themselves. Eventually, Red noticed a moving shadow behind a fractured column.

"It's alright," he voiced softly. "You can come out now."

After a moment of hesitation, Dawn shyly emerged from the rubble, stepping into the moonlight. Her tank-top dress was drenched in blood, and she was trembling with her hands nervously in the air. There was a certain mystique about her, a temperament well beyond her years.

"Are you gonna kill me?" she asked timidly.

"Put your hands down," Horse told her. "You're safe with us. We're the good guys."

"I know who you are," Dawn uttered, reluctant to cooperate. "…You're Soldiers."

Red looked upon her with pity in his heart, and neither confirmed nor denied her assertion.

"We're not here to hurt you," he said delicately. "Are you okay? You have any family out here? We can take you to them if you want."

Though she was silent, her eyes told the tale. After escaping an abusive father, she had been living on her own since the age of fourteen. She was in and out of foster homes and shelters, doing what she had to do to survive, and things only got worse after the earthquake. She learned all her lessons the hard way, and it left a massive chip on her shoulder.

Red wished he could more for her, but he was on a mission of grave importance. He removed his jacket, then gently tossed it to her as a gesture of mercy.

"Get out of here, kid," he sighed. "You deserve better than this."

Dawn caught the aviator jacket with both hands, somewhat bewildered. Shielding herself from the cold, she wrapped it around herself like a blanket, then noticed something was in the left pocket: it was a pearl-handled switchblade. Red walked away without another word, leading his men into a concrete abyss, and she watched them as they trekked deeper into darkness, until they vanished amongst the shadows of the late hour.

CHAPTER FOUR

Reloaded

All was quiet within the remains of Bunchy's Pawn Shop. Scattered winds danced through a massive breach in the wall, rolling over toppled shelves and scorched merchandise, carrying bright red embers in small gusts of debris. It had become a habitation of ghosts, a graveyard of nameless faces and cursed souls. Lifeless bodies were arranged in grand pools of vital fluids, like wet ornaments of flesh. In the corner of the demolished shop was an unassuming staircase, and behind that staircase was a secret bunker, hidden entirely from view.

Inside the bunker was a treasury of arms, a mighty arsenal, impressive by any standard. Racks of guns were next to shelves of ammunition in storage cages, while boxes of medical supplies were stacked and organized in industrial cabinets. Various blueprints for weapon upgrades were pinned against bulletin boards, and military shipping crates full of prototypes were arranged neatly on the concrete floor. Built for depository purposes, the everything-proof chamber was originally used for storing weapons and equipment, and served as a vital resource for the Stay Ready Soldiers. It was also the perfect refuge from a merciless war without end.

Laying atop a large sapele table, sprawled flat on his chest with a dressing wrapped around his leg, Bunchy slowly opened his eyes. All he could process was the pain surging through his entire body. He had a tremendous headache, his mouth was dry, and his thoughts were fragmented as he struggled to determine his own whereabouts. Completely disoriented, he gradually noticed a dark silhouette in the corner of the room. As he battled to regain focus, the blurred image eventually materialized into a man sitting on a stainless-steel worktable: it was Geronimo.

He had a blunt between his lips, carefully applying stitches to himself next to an open toolbox. With his shirt pulled up over his shoulder, exposing a multitude of scars on his arms and torso, and a bloody towel over his knee, strands of smoke cascaded through his nose as he glared at the needle, threading the flesh over his oblique muscle. Finally, he used his combat knife to cut to thread, then wiped away the remaining blood before taping a bandage over himself.

"I knew it," Bunchy murmured. "…I died and now I'm in hell."

Geronimo glanced at him with a warm expression on his face.

"I'd say you're about half right," he smirked.

"How long was I out?" Bunchy grumbled, rubbing his forehead.

"Not long enough, I'm afraid," Geronimo replied.

Suddenly, an unimaginable pain seized Bunchy, and he hollered out from the torturous sensation.

"What the shit!" he gritted, trying to crawl away.

"Hold still!" Kali yelled, pinning him down. "I almost got it!"

Twisting a set of tweezers into his shoulder, she latched onto a metallic sliver, then yanked the fragment from his body, causing blood to sprout from the wound like a jet stream.

"Holy fuck!" Bunchy shouted.

"Congratulations," Kali said proudly, dropping the lethal remnant on the table. "You'll live."

Drenched in sweat, Bunchy could feel the room starting to spin.

"Lucky me," he uttered between breaths.

Kali grabbed a clean towel, then dipped it in a mixing bowl of fresh water. She carefully cleaned the blood off his back with a soothing touch, then picked up a half-empty bottle of whiskey. She took a healthy swig, which puzzled Bunchy.

"I thought you quit drinking," he mumbled.

"I did," she grimaced.

She then poured the brown liquid over his wound, and he recoiled as if his back was on fire. Gripping the edges of the table with both hands, he shouted in agony as saliva flew from his mouth.

"There's antiseptic in the cabinet!" he scowled, eyes swelling with fury.

"Stop being a baby," Kali replied. "This is all I could find."

"Give me that!" Bunchy snarled, snatching the bottle from her hands. After taking a few breaths, he calmed himself down with a giant gulp of whiskey, embracing the burning sensation in his chest.

"At least the hard part's over," Kali smiled. "A couple stitches, and we're good to go."

"Perfect," said Bunchy, dropping his head in disapproval.

Geronimo quietly leaned against a support beam, flicking ashes from his blunt. As the leaf slowly disintegrated, he studied how Kali inserted the needle, and watched her carefully guide the thread diagonally over the wound, skillful enough to avoid any additional hemorrhaging. Meanwhile, Bunchy was trying to ignore the pain probing his back, gritting his teeth as he consumed more alcohol, launching him further into his own purgatory. Silently enduring the agony, his mind was afflicted with images of Samson's gruesome demise, impaling his soul with an indescribable emptiness. He could still hear him scream; he could still see the blood. Imprisoned by the lifeless eyes of his kin, he was incapable of escaping his own culpability. Each dose of liquor only festered his emotions, and when the guilt became undeniably overwhelming, he was ashamed of being alive.

When Geronimo finished the blunt, he squashed the smoky remnants beneath his boot, picked up a plastic vial of pills from the steel table, and ingested four white tablets at once without being noticed.

"Here, take these," he told Bunchy.

Bunchy glanced at the vial, then promptly declined.

"Nah, I'm good."

"It's just aspirin," Geronimo shrugged.

"No, it's not."

Geronimo raised an eyebrow, then carefully reviewed the prescription on the bottle.

"But it says aspirin right here..."

"It's Reaper Dust," Bunchy sighed. "It's a psychedelic. Real hallucinogenic shit."

Geronimo had a blank expression on his face, and did his best to hide his concern. He quietly walked over to the corner of the room, vexed and somewhat nervous. Although he was no stranger to drugs, he had never heard of a substance with such a name. However, rather than bring it to the forefront, he decided not to tell his comrades about the four tablets he had ingested, even though it was an honest mistake.

"You better be careful with that shit," Kali voiced.

"I honestly forgot I had it," Bunchy said with hesitation. "It used to be one of my many, many vices."

"But why your vices gotta say aspirin on it?" Geronimo blurted. "...Shit."

Bunchy and Kali glanced at him with a confused expression, puzzled by his outburst.

"Samson disapproved," Bunchy uttered eventually. "He was always preaching about eating right, and staying healthy... he was a fucking saint."

Geronimo could hear the pain in his voice, and refrained from speaking another word. As Kali concentrated on her work, she looked upon Bunchy with compassion and empathy.

"He meant a lot to all of us," she said softly.

Bunchy nodded somberly, fighting back the tears. He wanted to cry, he wanted to scream, he wanted to blow up the world. Loathsome and mournful, he was unable to escape the prison of his own torturous mind. Feeling a tap on his shoulder, he raised his head to see Geronimo standing over him, holding Samson's medallion. He delicately placed the blood-stained jewelry on the table as a humble gesture.

"He was a true Soldier," Geronimo told him. "One of the strongest men I've ever known. They'll never be another."

Bunchy picked up the necklace with a trembling hand, then silently held it in his palm. The chain was tangled, the link was broken, yet the medallion itself was unscathed. As he stared at the charm with a heavy heart, he raised the bottle of whiskey and poured a few drops to the floor. After a moment of silence, Geronimo was deep in thought as he leaned back against the support beam.

"If those fucking pigs hadn't ambushed us, we would've gotten here sooner," he said bitterly.

He walked over to an old computer positioned atop a small office desk. The outdated system was responsible for monitoring hidden cameras dispersed throughout the shop. The feed was still active, although a few cameras had been damaged in the firefight. Staring at the dusty screen, he was astounded by the numerous bodies in the ghostly wreckage.

"This is fucked up," he muttered, shaking his head. "For them to hit this place…"

"Red was right," Kali said ominously. "We've definitely been compromised."

According to Red, federal agents were already infiltrating various organizations, disrupting them from within, eliminating important leaders and prominent figures, then covering it up with propaganda and disinformation.

"That sounds about right," Bunchy slurred, unable to feel his lips.

Geronimo retrieved his trusty combat knife, then began pacing throughout the bunker in a meditative state, nonchalantly spinning it in his hand. As the shimmering blade swiftly rolled between and around his fingers, he methodically contemplated their next move.

"Speaking of Red, he'd probably want to know about this," he uttered.

Kali finished suturing, and delicately tied a knot in the thread. She dabbed Bunchy's back with another towel, then covered the stitches with two non-woven bandages. Afterward, she offered him a plastic bowl of clean water.

"Drink this," she insisted. "Slowly."

Bunchy accepted without hesitation, and long threads of cool liquid spilled from the corners of his mouth as he quickly guzzled the life-giving elixir.

"Or don't," she sighed, rolling her eyes.

Slightly revitalized, Bunchy dropped the bowl with a heavy belch.

"Hey, Moe," he coughed. "Before I forget, I got that order for you."

Geronimo stopped twirling his blade with a surprised expression.

"With everything going on, I figured it wasn't important," he said.

"Nah, fuck that," Bunchy declared, pointing toward a storage cage. "My word is bond, always."

Impressed by his resilience, Geronimo respectfully made his way past the padlocked entrance of the cage. Once inside, he was surrounded by black shelves stacked with metal drawers, each case filled with unique artillery designs. While admiring the possibilities, he noticed a simplex pistol-safe on an aluminum worktable, and butterflies fluttered in his stomach. He triggered the mechanical push-button lock, then slowly opened the pullout drawer.

Within the safe, twin customized Colt 1911 pistols were symmetrically displayed across charcoal foam, along with four extended magazines and a double back-draw holster. Originally, the weapons belonged to his grandfather, giving them an invaluable significance. Both carbon steel guns had the image of a tomahawk engraved on its slide, plus numerous symbols carved into the frames. With arrowheads etched in the grips and a deluxe blue finish, each pistol was a magnificent work of art.

"I got the specs like you wanted," Bunchy explained. "I treated the front straps and dehorned the frames, plus gave them trigger jobs. You got Magwells, compensators, ambidextrous thumb safeties, lasergrips, and fiber optic sights."

Geronimo selected one to study the modifications, and it was love at first sight. With his finger outside the trigger, he discharged the magazine and racked back the slide.

"And it ain't even my birthday," he grinned.

"I told you, my word's always bond," Bunchy insisted, propping himself on his elbows. "In fact, both of you should stock up on whatever you can. There's a duffel bag over there; knock yourselves out."

Kali was stunned, standing in disbelief. "No tax?" she questioned.

"It's the least I can do."

Geronimo and Kali glanced at each other with excitement in their eyes, then flew about the chamber in a whirlwind of reaching hands. They were like children in a candy store, each grabbing everything they could before Bunchy had the chance to change his mind. All around them were exceptional collections of gadgets, tactical equipment, and plenty of ammunition for the taking. It was Christmas and New Year's Eve at the same time. After gathering a lion's share of supplies, they were the epitome of America's worst nightmare.

Kali traded in her previous gear for a shemagh scarf, camouflaged cargo pants, assault boots, an assault vest with metal plates and grenades in the pouches, plus an M4A1 modified rifle. Geronimo was fully equipped in tactical boots, combat pants, assault gloves, and a tactical vest full of magazines under a black field jacket. With a duffel bag full of new weapons, and a freshly rolled blunt behind his ear, he was on top of the world.

"Hope I'm not forgetting anything," he said to himself.

"Wait a minute," Kali voiced. "Are we supposed to just walk out the front door? There's probably a dozen agents watching this place right now."

"Then we'll shoot our way out," Geronimo asserted.

"Don't be ignorant," Bunchy stated, sitting upright. "Help me move this table…"

While struggling to stand, he leaned upon Kali for support. Geronimo pushed the table back against the wall, uncovering a black ornate rug. Bunchy kicked the rug aside, revealing an iron trap door in the floor.

Kali was truly amazed. "You're just full of surprises," she declared.

"Figured this spot needed an emergency exit," Bunchy explained. "So, I installed a line into the mechanical tunnels."

Geronimo opened the latch and lifted the door, exposing a rusty ladder descending into a shadowy maze of metal.

"You gotta be shitting me," he mumbled.

Bunchy limped to the office desk, retrieved a bottle of bourbon and a pack of cigarettes from the bottom drawer, then painfully laid atop the steel surface.

"Those tunnels have been around for years," he added. "Just head west and you'll be fine."

"What're you doing?" Geronimo questioned.

Bunchy was entwined in his own mortality. "I think I'm done for the night," he mumbled, lighting a cancer stick on fire. "I'll only slow you down. You two get out of here…get as far away from this shit as you can…"

"Really?" Kali grilled. "You can't be serious."

Bunchy cracked a smile, clearly in pain. "You don't get it," he exhaled, venting clouds of smoke. "I'm through. I'm through with all of this…"

"What the fuck are you talking about?" Geronimo countered.

"Look at me," Bunchy stated. "I've given this enough of my life. I think I've earned some peace."

"This is crazy," Kali announced. "I know shit's bad. I get it. But we've all lost something in this war. You can't give up now."

"Listen, it ain't safe here," Geronimo said. "You're drunk, you've been shot, you're not thinking straight—"

"My cousin's dead, hear me!" Bunchy snapped. "I got nothing left! Everything's been taken from me! Fuck the police! Fuck the Soldiers! Fuck all of this shit! Only thing you guys ever did was fuck my life up!"

Geronimo was speechless, yet there was mercy in his brown eyes.

"Get out of here, Moe," sighed Bunchy. "Forget about me, alright? You can tell Red what you want, but I'm through…"

Geronimo shook his head, wishing he knew what to say. Speechless, he stared deep into the spiraling shadows of the trap door, dropped the bag of weapons down the shaft, then descended the ladder in absolute silence.

Kali stood in bewilderment, incapable of understanding why Bunchy was so willing to accept defeat. She was a natural born fighter, a true survivalist, and would rather die than surrender. However, she couldn't save him from himself.

Thus, she followed Geronimo down the rusty ladder, leaving Bunchy alone with his demons.

After reaching the concrete infrastructure below, she found herself in a narrow passageway, where the air was thick and humid. The walls were lined with air ducts, metal pipes, long cables, and colorful wires. Moths cavorted around flickering lights hanging from a corroded ceiling, while gnats gathered and danced in a thin blanket of haze. Waiting in the distance, Geronimo was reflecting on his own burdens. Plucking the blunt from behind his ear, he calmly sparked it aflame, then looked at Kali with a subtle tenderness. He quietly walked ahead into the mechanical maze, and she followed him without looking back.

CHAPTER FIVE

The Champion

In the dead of night, an intercity bus line was finally arriving at its destination. Passing the gates of a devoid terminal, the brakes whined as the wheels gradually rolled to a complete stop. Blue scatters of light from the station glimmered through the double-paned windows, dicing between dark spaces and empty shadows. Absolutely exhausted, a greying operator named Barry leaned back in his worn seat with a heavy sigh, thankful to reach the end of a long shift. Glancing at the overhead mirror, he hardly recognized himself due to the heavy luggage under his bloodshot eyes.

He pushed a lever to open the sliding doors, then happily turned off the engine.

"Last stop," he declared, looking over his shoulder.

He was disappointed to see a single passenger sleeping at the end of the bus.

"Last stop!" he repeated with more assurance.

After no response, he stood up and slowly made his way down the isle of empty seats, too tired to be angry.

Approaching the lone traveler, he could hear the distinct sound of snoring getting louder and louder.

"Sir, it's time to wake up," he said with an artificial smile.

Sprawled across the entire back row, the passenger had his feet on the seats and his head against the window. His hair was wild and unkempt, and a visible trail of drool caught the light as it dampened the collar of his shirt. Wearing a pair of black cowboy boots and a bomber jacket, he had a gold pendant that hung loosely around his neck, and a pair of aviator sunglasses over his eyes.

"Sir, please wake up," Barry requested, shaking the man by the shoulder. Unfortunately, the snoring only persisted, and he was forced to consider a more aggressive approach. He stood over the sleeping passenger, and carefully leaned next to his ear.

"Wake the fuck up!" he shouted.

Startled from his slumber, the traveler immediately seized Barry by the throat. As Barry struggled for his life, the mysterious man calmly lowered his sunglasses, then took a moment to survey the empty bus. He eventually released his grip, and Barry collapsed to the floor, gasping for air. The man stood up, stretched his arms high above his head, then began cracking various joints in his upper body. His name was Dirt, and he was Minister of Foreign Affairs for the SRS.

"Sorry about that," he yawned. "Loud noises make me nervous."

Barry was panting on his hands and knees, happy to be alive.

"That's understandable," he said between breaths.

Dirt looked out the window and stared at the city lights beyond the barren railway tracks.

"So, this is it, huh?" he asked, adjusting his jacket.

Barry nodded as he sat on the floor.

"Welcome to LA," he groaned, rubbing his larynx.

"Beautiful," Dirt smiled.

He helped Barry to his feet, apologetically brushed off his wrinkled uniform, then concluded the awkward exchange with a brief hug.

"You know, I feel good about this," he grinned, patting Barry on the back. "I think we made a real connection here."

Dazed and confused, Barry inelegantly nodded, then Dirt gently pushed him aside before politely exiting the bus.

"This town's really gone to shit," Barry grumbled to himself.

Dirt stepped outside onto a concrete platform, embracing the cool night air. Steel columns supported a giant canopy overhead, and a small sequence of vacant buses were parked in designated spaces. Corroded tracks separated the station from the rest of the city, while surrounding buildings towered over the vast complex. The isolated terminal was virtually deserted, and he could hear his own footsteps echo off the pavement as he walked across the immense lot and beyond the gates.

He soon found himself alone in the misty streets, navigating a realm of nocturnal landscapes. Rippling puddles reflected the majesty of a crimson moon, floating in an obsidian sky. Functioning streetlights were scarce, paving the avenues with darkness. Thistles were sprouting from cracks and crevices, and surrounding structures had boards nailed over the windows. His path was a combination of multiple twists and turns that took him up dusky hills, down dismal alleyways, over fields of concrete, and around lonely forgotten corners.

In the silent twilight of the city, he retracted a hip flask from his jacket, and helped himself to a sip of warm bourbon. The air horn from a distant locomotive made him look toward the glowing skyline of downtown, and he eventually remembered how much he despised walking. After journeying beneath a stack interchange of connecting highways and bridges, he found himself staring at the stoned surface of a massive retaining wall.

"Look at that," he uttered, standing in awe.

There it was, shining in the light of the moon: a remarkable mural of Tree Newman, the founder of the Stay Ready Soldiers. The portrait managed to capture specific details, and the likeness was eerily uncanny. The graphic illustration included his trademarked black beanie, horn-rimmed glasses, and patchy beard. His facial expression had his signature intensity, and in the backdrop was a red sky opening dramatically above his head. With a giant black tree growing from a city in ruins, "*Stay Ready Soldiers*" was written in capital letters, and "*Freedom Justice Equality*" was tagged underneath it.

It was incredibly inspiring to see the mural, and Dirt was captivated by the striking image. In a short span of time, Tree managed to establish many core principles, such as the value of identity, the power of awareness, and the gift of self-reliance. It was the knowledge he instilled in his followers that molded them into true Soldiers.

Dirt remained frozen in place, mesmerized by the colors, overpowered by emotion, and in the bourbon-soaked corners of his mind, he recalled a very specific conversation they shared. It was shortly after someone firebombed Tree's hotel room in Culver City, right before everything changed…

...A few months ago, in the Crenshaw district, Tree Newman was on a rooftop sitting at an aluminum table. Next to a bag of ganja and a bottle of cognac, he flicked a few ashes and exhaled a cloud of smoke high into the atmosphere. The sky was a fusion of red and gold behind the setting sun, washing the broken buildings in a magnificent blanket of warm colors. Birds flocked in unison over the horizon, and the surrounding palm trees fluttered peacefully in the calm wind. While staring in the distance, one of his bodyguards—a heavy-handed man by the name of Victor—interrupted his serenity. "That cowboy lookin' motherfucker is here to see you."

Still gazing at the sky, Tree did his best not to laugh.

"Just the man I wanted to see," he smiled.

Though his brow exposed his disapproval, Victor nodded in compliance, then marched to the access door at the far end of the roof. After opening the steel hatch, Dirt walked past him with a scowl on his face.

"I should throw your ass off this building," he threatened, pointing at Victor. "You're lucky I'm a peaceful man."

Victor scoffed at him in disgust. "I'd love to see you try that," he said with his chest out.

"Then maybe you should stick around," Dirt replied, clenching his fists.

Victor's blood began to boil, but he swallowed his pride for the sake of his position. He angrily made his exit through the access door, intent on returning to his post.

"Stay the fuck out of my face," he said over his shoulder. "You'll live longer."

After he left, Dirt brushed it off as another pointless interaction. Although he was hardly a fan of people, there was something about Victor he truly detested. He turned around with a foul taste in his mouth, then walked toward the man he considered a friend.

47

Tree could barely hide his amusement as he poured himself a quarter pint of cognac. "Peace, Soldier," he grinned.

Shaking his head, Dirt pulled up a chair at the table. "Where'd you find that clown?" he grumbled. "Making me wait twenty minutes; that's just rude."

"Relax, brother," Tree answered lightheartedly. "He's cool..."

Apparently, Victor was another casualty of society, another leftover raised by the gutters and back alleyways. He supposedly had an extensive rap sheet, including everything from vandalism to armed robbery, and after frequenting the penitentiary for most of his life, he somehow managed to cross paths with Tree Newman himself, becoming his personal bodyguard.

"I never liked him," said Dirt. "He's all attitude and no personality."

"This is true," Tree smiled, passing him the blunt.

Dirt quietly shook his head as he accepted the burning leaf, then slowly inhaled the medicine. After filling his lungs to their maximum capacity, he exhaled a massive smoke cloud over the horizon. "Some kid asked about the food program the other day," he said eventually. "I had to tell him we don't do things like that anymore."

Tree paused solemnly, reflecting on the inescapable nightmare he created. "But did you tell him why? Did you tell him those devils had the audacity to firebomb a youth center? If your brother hadn't been there...people would've been burying their children."

With the weight of the world on his shoulders, he was starting to feel the pressure. Fighting against government tyranny and oppression, his ability to convey ideas and incite change was exactly why the establishment feared him. There was a bounty on his head, and no one he could trust.

"Shit, I can't even sleep now without a pistol next to me," Tree added.

Dirt nodded as he passed him the burning leaf. "Keep the faith, brother," he said. "You got angels watching over you."

"I hope so, because the devil's trying to kill me," Tree countered, putting the blunt to his lips. "A lot of people think I started this war, but they don't know shit. None of them do. I'm out here fighting for them, and now I'm the bad guy."

As gray strands of smoke dispersed in the wind, Dirt spotted a red-tailed hawk gliding majestically over the falling sun. "How far is this gonna go?" he voiced, envying the hawk.

"Depends on how far they wanna take it."

With a sigh, Dirt pulled a personalized flask from his pocket, then gulped down a healthy portion of brown liquor. "So, it's a pissing contest now," he winced.

"Nah, pride makes you careless," Tree stated. "It's bigger than that. The whole damn system's corrupt. I know you see it; we all see it. And I hate to break it to you, but all that marching and singing ain't gonna change shit." He released a trail of smoke from his nostrils, then handed off the cigarillo.

After plucking the blunt from his fingertips, Dirt inhaled the potion as a plane flew overhead. "So, what's the endgame?" he asked, envying the plane. "Tell me. Is it when they got tanks rolling up the street? Or drones shooting you from the sky? We're talking about a whole goddamn army."

"Damn right," said Tree. "We're all behind enemy lines. Everyone's in the trenches, even if they don't know it yet. This country's a prison for people like us. If you really want change, you have to bleed for it. Reality isn't always pretty. That's why I wanted to talk to you, because certain things are about to happen. You've always been one of my top Soldiers, Dirt. You and your brother. You're both strong, you're both honest, and I need you both standing with me for the next phase."

As silver strings of smoke tangled and evaporated, Dirt calmly wiped the ashes from his shirt. "You already know where we stand," *he asserted.* "I just hope you got a plan to go with that pretty speech of yours."

Tree stroked his beard with a smile. "Yeah, try not to die," *he chuckled.*

Minutes melted into hours as they conversed over endless smoke. This exchange of ideas was an established routine, based on a level of trust and respect developed over time and space. As the ganja dissolved, and the sun gradually descended from view, Dirt could see the same hawk from earlier, soaring through a purple sky...

...After their conversation on the roof, Tree proved to be a man of his word, and launched a violent crusade against the LAPD. In retaliation for all the injustice and brutality, he coordinated successful strikes on courthouses and police stations, ultimately turning the city into a war zone. In the end, he was respected, feared, loved, and condemned.

Standing beneath the crimson moon, Dirt poured out a taste of liquor in remembrance. Suddenly, something moved in his peripheral vision. When he turned around, he was surprised to see a young man in his early twenties. He had pink and bleached-blonde hair, with a dusty jean jacket over a grungy tank top. Holding an aerosol can full of paint, he casually approached the mural, and began tagging over it with graffiti.

"What the fuck are you doing?" Dirt barked at him.

The colorful-haired stranger paused momentarily. "What the fuck does it look like?" he shrugged, shaking the can.

"Go somewhere else with that shit! This wall's off limits!"

"Says who?" scoffed the young man, eyeing him up and down. "Are you the police or somethin'?"

"Don't insult me. Now get out of here before I make you eat that spray can."

The blonde was almost stunned. "Are we making threats now?" he scowled.

Helping himself to one last drink, Dirt tipped back the flask until it was completely empty, then wiped his chin before sealing the cap. "You're right. I'm a little drunk, and that was rude of me," he acknowledged. "Tag that shit someplace else, please. You should have more respect for the dead."

"Fuck you," the youngster laughed. "Wearing sunglasses at night. Who the hell does that?"

With a sigh, Dirt shook his head as he stepped forward. "I'm not telling you again," he warned.

The young man looked at him sideways, still amused. He tossed the spray can aside, then quickly pulled out a switchblade from his back pocket. "Or what?" he countered, walking toward him.

It was a disappointing sight from Dirt's perspective. "Wow," he said, crossing his arms. "You're really doing this…"

The hooligan flashed him a sinister grin. "Here's the deal," he said, clearing his throat. "You give up the chain, and your wallet, and I'll do what I came here to do. We can act like this never happened. I'll even let you keep those fancy-ass boots."

"You like these?"

"Why would anyone like those?" he responded, waving the cheap blade in dissent. "Now shut the hell up and give me your shit, before I change my mind."

Dirt was already calculating his next move. "Listen up, cowboy," he said in a steady tone. "I can tell you're not as smart as you look. So, I need you to focus. Do yourself a favor; walk away. You got your whole life ahead of you, and I'd hate to fuck you up over some silly shit like this."

After a brief silence, the blonde started laughing hysterically.

"Are you shitting me?" he exclaimed. "I'm the one with the fucking knife!"

Dirt took another step forward. "Check this out, blondie," he said. "I got places to be. So, to sum it up, take your ass back to Hollyweird, before I stamp this wall with your face."

The stranger glared at him in disbelief. "You talk a lot of shit," he snarled. "Maybe I should cut out your tongue."

In a flash, he lunged directly at Dirt's jugular with his knife extended. However, Dirt swiftly deflected the strike with his flask, swatting the blade to the pavement. The thug jumped backward with wide eyes, clutching his wrist in pain. Dirt peacefully opened his arms to offer a truce, yet the young man refused to be deterred. Standing nervously still, his eyes swayed toward the feeble weapon at his feet.

"Don't do it," Dirt told him, reading his mind. "You can walk away right now. No harm; no foul. But, if you go for that knife, I can't help you."

Feeling anxious, the young man disregarded the advice. He darted for the knife, but Dirt swiftly intercepted his path by stomping hard on his shoe, pinning his foot to the ground. The blonde hollered in pain as his toes were crushed, then attempted to push Dirt off balance. However, Dirt countered his maneuver with a powerful forearm, and knocked him to the earth while standing firmly on his foot. The youngster had the pleasure of hearing his own tibia snap as his back landed on the pavement. He let out a deafening scream, horrified by the sight of his shinbone piercing the skin.

"Tough break," said Dirt, spitting on the blacktop.

Suddenly, a forty-ounce bottle of malt liquor flew past his head and shattered against the mural. He slowly turned around to see three more hooligans standing in the distance. One of them had green dreadlocks, and he boldly stepped forward with bravado in his voice.

"Hey!" he shouted. "What'd you do to him?"

Dirt looked around innocently. "Who?" he shrugged. "You mean Happy Feet over here?"

Another ruffian wearing skinny jeans was holding a red Louisville Slugger. "You're so fucking dead!" he hollered, pointing the bat menacingly.

Dirt was beginning to feel like the butt of a bad joke. "Listen, fellas," he said apathetically. "I sense a lot of aggression here, so we should all take a deep breath and calm down. We can talk this out like adults."

After he spoke, the thug gripping the baseball bat rushed him at full speed. Intensity was in his eyes as he swung with all his might, aiming for Dirt's head. However, Dirt easily blocked the assault with one hand, then instantly struck the youngster in his elbow, snapping it backward. The skinny-jeaned gangster buckled over as he fumbled the bat, his distorted arm hanging like a broken wing. Before he could process the pain, Dirt picked up the Louisville Slugger and connected with his temple for a grand slam.

The bat was glistening with blood as he tossed it aside, and the last two louts glanced at each other nervously. Eventually, the one with green dreadlocks gathered up enough courage to charge into battle. He hollered as he launched a flurry of amateur kicks and punches, imitating every action movie he studied on television. Too fast to be touched, Dirt swiftly seized him by the throat, lifted him off his feet, then slammed him on his back in brutal fashion. Afterward, Dirt grabbed him by the head, and bounced it ferociously atop the concrete. He stood to his feet, cracked his knuckles, then casually approached the last man with a scowl on his face.

Cringing with fright, the young man was shaking in his designer sneakers. "Don't hurt me!" he stammered. "I just met those guys! I barely know them!"

Dirt grabbed him by the collar of his polyester jacket. "You should find better friends," he said. He planted a massive headbutt between the eyes, knocking the hooligan unconscious, then watched his body slump to the ground like a ragged doll. Silence fell upon the land, and Dirt stood tall in the moonlight as a gust of wind wrapped around him. He took a deep breath, wiped the blood from his brow, then stepped over the youngster in a huff.

"This town really has gone to shit," he mumbled, continuing his journey.

CHAPTER SIX

The Beast

All was virtually silent as the armored convoy navigated a dark and barren wasteland. As pale cones of light emanated from slanted streetlamps, the carrier roamed over piles of debris, crushing stacks of rubble down to grains of sand. Inside the war machine, members of the Black Hawk Battalion were growing impatient. Anxious for battle, Rico had his eyes closed, utilizing the biochip implant in his brain stem. He had access to a virtual library of highly sensitive data, including classified files on the Stay Ready Soldiers. He was analyzing their infrastructure, combing archives of photographs and pseudonyms. He studied their ten-point program, their rules of engagement, their solidarity with youth organizations, and their anti-establishment doctrines.

Hennessy glanced at him, fascinated by his hypnotic state. "Hey, Rico," he said discretely. "…What's it like?"

Rico's eyes fluttered open, then he reluctantly turned toward his comrade. "What do you mean?" he murmured.

"Seriously? You were gone for months, and they never told us anything. We didn't know what they were doing to you."

Rico stared solemnly ahead. "I don't know what they did to me either," he alluded. "I don't dream anymore. That's something I have noticed. But, other than that, I honestly feel great."

"If you say so," Hennessy replied. "I can't believe you went along with that shit."

"What's so hard to believe? I'm stronger, I'm faster—"

"Yeah, but how much of you…is still you?" Hennessy questioned. "You ever think about that?"

Rico looked down at his hands. "Nope, too busy kicking ass," he smirked.

Meanwhile, Dozer was slouched in his seat, watching a mandatory advertisement on his tablet:

"Are you sad? Lonely? Depressed? Do you have trouble sleeping at night, or problems waking up in the morning? Are you stressed, bald, and overweight? Do people hate you? Has your penis stopped working? Here at Core Pharmaceuticals, we understand that life can be a painful existence, full of disappointment and regret. That's why Norilex is here to help. Imagine, all of life's problems, solved by a single pill."

"Who buys this shit?" Dozer criticized.

"Remember, when taking Norilex, do not drive or operate heavy machinery. Side effects include headaches, dizziness, changes in behavior; confusion, paranoia, hallucinations; suicidal thoughts, heart-attack, stroke; bloody diarrhea, paralysis, decapitation, and frostbite. So, ask your doctor if Norilex is right for you. From Core Pharmaceuticals, a subsidiary of Hydricore."

When the commercial was over, Dozer was officially disgusted. After an additional low-budget advertisement for a local gun shop, he was relieved to see the initial program return:

"*Welcome back to* Society Today. *I am your host, Rudolph Scott. Here at the Core News Network, we take pride in addressing the issues others are afraid to touch. That's why it brings me great pleasure to introduce the man himself, the one responsible for protecting our great city: police chief Andrew Bryson. Chief, are you with us?*"

The screen spliced in two, simultaneously broadcasting Andrew Bryson through a remote satellite feed. Wearing a black sports coat over a casual shirt, the balding chief was looking straight ahead with cold eyes.

"*I'm here, Scott,*" *he said.*

"*It's truly an honor, sir,*" *Rudolph smiled.* "*Thanks for joining us. I know you're a busy man. And with everything that's happening, we're glad to see you're in good health.*"

Bryson lifted his chin proudly. "*Yes, at the moment, me and my family are relatively safe,*" *he declared.* "*It'll take more than some measly fire to get rid of me.*"

"*Good to hear,*" *said Rudolph, adjusting his collar.* "*So, let's get into it. According to a recent poll on social media: citizens are terrified, now more than ever. The violence in this city has grown exponentially, especially over the past year, and people are afraid to leave their homes. What are your thoughts about this?*"

Bryson cleared his throat before he answered. "*Well, we're living in an era of maniacs shooting up schools and churches,*" *he stated.* "*It's a disease.*"

"*Interesting,*" *Rudolph noted.* "*At yesterday's press conference, you made some rather strong statements concerning the Stay Ready Soldiers. You also eluded that we're on the verge of martial law. Now, I know many conservatives have come out in your support. But there are some critics who disagree with your...tactics. Any thoughts?*"

"My critics are part of the problem," Bryson told him. "My tactics? Please. We're the ones standing between order and chaos; we're the ones protecting you from yourselves. Our job is to keep the peace, and it's the most dangerous job in the world. We put our lives on the line every day for this city—"

"But when officers are caught on camera shooting unarmed civilians, there's bound to be some backlash," Rudolph explained. "How many people have been killed by police this year alone? We're only in July, and nineteen deaths have already been recorded. Most recently, a fourteen-year-old boy. Is this what you call keeping the peace?"

Bryson didn't even flinch. "I never said it was easy," he replied. "But I find it interesting that no one ever complains when a police officer gets killed. Where's the backlash for that? What about our children, our families? Like I said, we put our lives on the line every day."

"Sir, I recognize that your job isn't easy," Rudolph insisted. "And we do mourn for those officers who've sacrificed their lives. But let's be honest, people don't trust the police anymore. And instead of trying to reestablish that trust, you've literally declared war."

"I've declared war on the scum that's tearing this city apart," Bryson countered. "Anyone threatening the growth and development of a peaceful Los Angeles."

"You're talking about the SRS?"

"Of course," Bryson nodded.

"I see," said Rudolph, stroking his chin. "At that same press conference, you said you planned on completely eradicating the SRS, and their supporters."

"Absolutely," Bryson said sternly. "The Stay Ready Soldiers are nothing more than a terrorist group. They're a bunch of ex-cons and hoodlums, a syndicate of anarchists with delusions of grandeur.

They've killed officers in cold blood, they've bombed police stations, they've endangered people's lives. Everyone needs to stop glorifying them like they're a bunch of patriots."

"No one's glorifying anything, believe me," Rudolph replied. "What about those who say that the Soldiers have also implemented radical socioeconomic programs? Things like free food, clothing, shelter, and medicine? Some say they're an alternative to our society's current social structure."

"I just told you they're a terrorist organization. Ask yourself. How'd they get the food in the first place? Where did they get the clothes and the medicine? They hijack supply lines at gunpoint; nothing patriotic about that. And their free programs are just recruitment camps for other low-life punks. They're a collection of blood-thirsty savages. Stop putting them on a pedestal."

"No one's doing that here," Rudolph asserted. "Let's move on. What about the recent allegations of you accepting bribes to implement a 'shoot-first' policy in low-income neighborhoods? Is there any truth to this?"

Bryson was taken aback, though he disguised it well beneath a stern demeanor. "Scott, listen to yourself," he scoffed. "You're starting to sound like one of those conspiracy theorists that still live in their parents' basement. My only concern has always been the safety and well-being of our citizens. My job is to maintain law and order; period. There's no hidden agenda here."

Rudolph suddenly placed his index finger against his earpiece. "Right," he sighed. "Unfortunately, my producer is telling me it's time for a commercial break. So, don't go anywhere. We'll be right back."

The program quickly cut to a strange advertisement for a florescent blue-colored energy drink.

⊷═◍

Beneath the City of Angels, an underground network of more than two hundred known tunnels stretched for miles in every direction. According to legend, this complex system had numerous functions aside from running pipes, wires, and cables. Theories ranged from an abandoned transit system, to an entire subterranean culture hidden within the mysterious labyrinth of steel and cement. There were tales of the grid being used to convey liquor during the age of prohibition, as well as horror stories of police using the intricate pathways for transporting criminals to secret death camps. Many corridors and passageways were closed off by private organizations and government officials for undisclosed purposes. Not only was public access forbidden, it was decreed punishable by the state to the furthest extent of the law.

Nevertheless, Geronimo and Kali were making their way through one of the lost service tunnels. Bursts of steam sprouted from various valves attached to expansive pipelines branching along the walls, shrouding the ominous warning signs that remained plastered against the concrete. Rats and roaches scattered from their approaching footsteps, and the chamber was sweltering with unbearable heat.

Kali heard the crunch of an insect under her shoe. "Remind me to burn these boots," she mumbled.

"There's worse things down here than roaches," said Geronimo in a serious tone. "Could be giant alligators."

Kali raised an eyebrow at the thought. "Alligators?"

"Or reptilians," Geronimo shrugged. "You never know; I try to keep an open mind."

Kali swatted at a fluttering moth. "If you're trying to scare me, it's not working," she lied. "Besides, I could use a new purse."

Continuing their odyssey through the iron caverns, they advanced further into uncharted territory. They trekked deeper into the automated substructure, navigating through a network of shadowy twists and turns, in an artificial maze that appeared to be endless. Elaborate spiderwebs lingered in suspension, while crawling creatures of all kinds receded into the dark crevices of the foundation. Droplets of water from the ceiling evaporated quickly within the confined passageways, and mold from the moisture made the air stale and suffocating.

Sweating from the extreme temperature, Kali feared the prospect of being trapped in an unyielding mechanical web, doomed to wander aimlessly forever. As the severe heat intensified, it appeared as if they were going in circles. However, while progressing through yet another graffiti-covered corridor boasting occult symbolism, she noticed Geronimo was oddly calm. She was used to him maintaining a certain disposition, a level of composure that was set in stone. Still, he was acting much more reserved than usual.

"Hey, you okay?" she asked.

Geronimo tried reassuring her with a slight grin, and though his poise was steadfast, he was beginning to feel the effects of the Reaper Dust. As the trip gradually progressed, he noticed his heart rate had rapidly increased, and he was experiencing abrupt lapses in time.

"Moe, what's wrong?" Her words were distorted and inaudible, as if she were talking underwater, yet Geronimo maintained his silent demeanor.

Fighting desperately to concentrate, a dark fog emerged, and his mind was engulfed in a liquid static. His equilibrium became unbalanced, and the sound of his heart pounding against his chest soon amplified, resonating a continuous high-pitched tone in his right ear. Moving in slow motion, his grip on reality nullified with each step. As he walked through an everlasting corridor, pixelated shadows began sliding across the floor, like dark waves on an ocean surface.

Staggering in a haze, the ground beneath his feet became the soft currents in a river of mercury. Fragments of light curled into smoke, and walls ignited into bright emerald flames. The ceiling rippled and dissolved, forming a black basin overhead that coiled into the far reaches of ubiquity. Obstructions in his path unraveled, expanding the chamber until it was boundless in space. Standing on an endless plane of rushing water, he felt weightless and unrestrained, mesmerized by the vision.

However, Kali was nowhere in sight. He called out for her, yet was unable to make a sound. Instead, a single bubble of air floated from his mouth, and spiraled into the infinite void unfolding around him. Doubting where to turn, he looked down at the water flowing continuously in all directions, and noticed his reflection upon the surface was smiling back at him.

Suddenly, thunder rolled in the darkness, then a fantastic cloud of fire manifested deep within the aqueous sky. With brilliant flames of gold enveloping upon itself, the cloud began drifting toward him, shining radiantly amid tangling shadows. He remained fixated on its magnificence, marveling at its beauty, and a pleasurable sensation gently washed over his entire body.

Then, the waters around him began to swell and reconstruct. Dividing into black columns of liquid, they dramatically mutated, forming anthropomorphic creatures.

Rising from the murky depths of the unexplained, they appeared by the multitudes, warping and arcing with the waves. One would rise to consume another, a process that ensued repetitively, until the aquatic beings focused on Geronimo. As if alerted by his presence, they violently ripped through each other in a savage attempt to reach his location.

He retained his fortitude as they surrounded him, standing fearless among the faceless monstrosities. Their clutches remained inches away, as if repelled by an invisible force, giving him a sudden realization of ordained power. The creatures moved as he moved, never compromising the space between them. Thus, he began walking toward the miraculous cloud of fire in the sky, maneuvering safely through the ravenous pack of ferocious beasts.

Staring at the luminous vapor, red lightning bolts erupted within the expanding inferno, and an immense monolith of crystal appeared from behind the flames. With the creatures lingering at bay, his steps slowly elevated, as if he reached an escalator made entirely of air. The enormous prism above emanated flares of light, and became transparent as he floated toward its lucid exterior. In a state of inspiration, he began swimming upwards through the atmosphere, beyond the event horizon. Soaring close enough to touch the crystallized surface, he could see past the window to the other side, into a fantasy world of alluring green pastures that beckoned for his return.

He instantly heard a soft voice from the heavens. "Open the door," it said.

The watery creatures collapsed as Geronimo stretched toward the ever-fluctuating crystal.

"Open the door," the voice repeated.

His hand pressed against the outer shell, causing an oscillating effect that pulsated throughout the firmament.

"Open the door!" Kali yelled.

In the blink of an eye, Geronimo found himself standing in front of a metallic access door. After unknowingly leading Kali through the mechanical underground, he was now gripping an iron handwheel that was firmly locked in place. She was sweating profusely behind him, impatiently waiting for him to open the hatch.

"Why are you just standing there?" she criticized, jabbing him in the back. "Open the damn door!"

Turning the rustic wheel, Geronimo heard the bolts unlock, then used his shoulder to forcefully unseal the entryway. As a gust of cool air rushed into the chamber, Kali felt a surge of relief. She shoved him aside, then eagerly stepped through the door, entering the damp belly of an enclosed bridge. Absent of any substantial light, the ground was covered in a primordial moss, and the surrounding walls were blanketed in the usual graffiti. Allowing the breeze to soothe her delicate skin, she headed straight for the concrete steps, ascending to the surface.

Still recovering from his incredible experience, Geronimo was dumbfounded, scratching his head in a bewilderment of wonder and curiosity. The kaleidoscope of images and emotions dominated his psyche, compelling him to contemplate its meaning. He cautiously exited through the hatch, then carefully closed the door behind him, leaving the mysterious tunnels in the dark, along with all its perplexing secrets.

CHAPTER SEVEN

Hard Lessons

Beneath a layer of endless night, the scarlet moon remained idle in a firmament of darkness. As time slowly approached the witching hour, a troubled youth was standing outside a local convenience store, crooning at the top of his lungs. The neon glow of a bright insignia radiated above the shop's entrance, serving as a spotlight for his late-night performance. His name was Anthony, though everyone called him Ant. With a prominent bruise across his cheekbone, his jacket was torn and soiled with filth, and his left hand was wrapped in a green cast. Swaying to an unknown rhythm in his head, singing was a therapeutic process for his soul. Although some words were indecipherable, every note was gracefully harmonic. He had the voice of a celestial being.

"Kid, you're killing me," someone complained.

With his mantra disrupted, the lowly vagabond turned around, then politely waved at the shopkeeper standing in the doorway.

"Mr. Daniels," he smiled, flashing a silver canine tooth. "How's your night going?"

Mr. Daniels carefully surveyed the street, then reluctantly stepped out into the elements. "Wonderful," he frowned. "You've been out here singing for the past hour, and you're literally repelling all of my customers."

Anthony held out his arms in an inquisitive manner, accentuating the obvious. "What customers?" he asked innocently.

"Exactly. Now take that Motown shit across the street."

Though he was still smiling, Anthony was hiding his disappointment. "It's good to see a love for the arts is still present in this thriving society of ours."

"Stop, I've always supported your singing," the shopkeeper groaned. "It's just…I worry about you sometimes. Why don't you stay at the shelter?"

"It's not so much a shelter, really. It's more like a Nazi death camp."

"Jesus, are you always this dramatic?" Mr. Daniels voiced, shaking his head. He retracted a small knot of wrinkled money from his pocket. "Here, get yourself some breakfast on me," he said, offering the soul singer a fifty-dollar bill.

Anthony happily slid the paper in his cast, then bowed gracefully to show his gratitude. "I will accept your tribute, good sir," he said. "And I shall honor your request."

With pity in his heart, Mr. Daniels returned his gesture with a subtle smile. "Whatever you say, kid," he sighed, returning to his shop.

Anthony watched as the door closed, longing for somewhere far from this reality. Isolated in a city of despair, he trotted meekly across the empty street, then retreated to a dark and pungent alleyway. He leaned against a dumpster with a sorrowful heart, and started singing yet again, finding refuge within the rift of his own psyche. However, his harmony was cut short when a clatter arose from the darkness. With goosebumps on the back of his neck, he stood perfectly still as a mysterious figure materialized from a nearby lake of shadows.

"Who's there?" he blurted out.

After a tense silence, Dawn emerged with the demeanor of a small pup, exhausted from walking all night. With Red's bomber jacket clutched tightly around her shoulders, her mind was in a million different places, spanning throughout time and space, summoning emotions she was afraid to explore.

"You shouldn't sneak around like that," Anthony expressed, relieved to see a friendly face. "You have no idea how stressful that was."

Dawn was still recovering from her experience at the Forum. "Good to see you, too," she said, putting on a plastic smile.

"Nice jacket," Anthony noticed, scratching his head. "What're you doing out here? Why aren't you at the shelter?"

"I could ask you the same thing," she countered.

"True, but I asked you first."

Dawn looked down at the ground, reflecting on her choices in life, then eventually shrugged her shoulders in indifference.

"Who cares…that place is full of weirdos."

"This whole town's full of weirdos," Anthony sighed.

"Yeah," she thought aloud. "I fucking hate LA."

Anthony glared at the crimson moon, envisioning a lost time, and a forgotten land. "It wasn't always like this," he explained. "Things used to be different; people used to look out for each other…"

"Prove it," she sneered.

"I'm not saying shit was great, but everything changed after that earthquake. There're still good people out there. You just have to give them a chance."

Dawn gave him a dirty look as she sucked her teeth. "Is that what happened to you?" she grilled, pointing at his cast. "You gave somebody a chance?"

Anthony quickly tucked his arm under his coat, somewhat embarrassed. "I'm starting a new fashion trend," he replied timidly.

"Please," she said in a serious tone. "Who was it?"

"Nobody," he replied, trying to play it off. "It's nothing, really…"

"Don't tell me it's that same cop," she grumbled.

Anthony stood with a helpless expression, revealing the truth in his silence. His wrist had been fractured in three places, due to a recent encounter with a sadistic officer, who had been routinely harassing him over the past few weeks. From overnight stints in jail, to outright physical attacks, the crooked lawman enjoyed watching him suffer, and the assaults were only getting worse.

"What's with that guy?" Dawn hissed. "Why's he always fucking with you?"

"I wish I knew," Anthony voiced. "Maybe I'm too pretty."

"The prettiest," she added with half a smile.

"You get it," he grinned.

Dawn folded her arms, then slowly paced in circles by the dumpster, calculating a solution. "So, what should we do about it?" she finally asked.

Anthony responded with a puzzled expression. "What do you mean?" he shrugged. "It's not like I can call the cops."

"...We could kill him," she suggested.

Anthony paused for a moment, then laughed robustly at the notion. "Of course. Brilliant. Why didn't I think of that?"

"I'm serious," she spoke coldly. "Why the hell not?"

"Um, let me think," he chuckled. "Because it's crazy? Does that sound about right?"

"Whatever," she mumbled, staring at a passing plane.

⋆──◉

As fate would have it, a fatigued Dirt just so happened to wander upon that very same block. On a quest to quench his thirst, he promptly entered Mr. Daniels' convenience store. A brass bell chimed as he opened the door, and a distinct odor caught his attention once he stepped inside. Behind the counter, Mr. Daniels was casually holding a shotgun.

"Evening," he declared. "Can I help you?"

Dirt innocently raised his hands with an easy grin. "Top of the morning to you," he said. "I'm just here for a drink; no need for hostility."

Mr. Daniels calmly tapped the barrel. "I don't want any trouble," he smiled.

Dirt casually dropped his hands, then proceeded toward the refrigerator aisle with his eye on the shopkeeper. The store was dreary and rundown, with dusty shelves and yellow floors covered in grime. Whistling an old tune, he grabbed a twenty-four ounce can of beer, then calmly approached the register. He placed the can on the faded countertop, then nodded informally toward the shotgun.

"Nice Remington," he said. "You use it a lot?"

"Is that a trick question?" Mr. Daniels scoffed. "Between the thugs trying to rob me, and the cops trying to extort me?

Brother, I'm my own security. Shit. It's a miracle I'm still in business."

Before Dirt could respond, he was distracted by a row of cigarettes behind the counter. Feeling the sweat in his palms, he was standing in the valley of decision, face-to-face with his greatest challenge. It was a rendezvous with destiny at the crossroads.

Mr. Daniels cleared his throat. "Anything else?"

Dirt made his exit after setting his money on the counter. Once he was outside, he quickly popped open the can of beer, and immediately regretted buying the cigarettes.

⋯⊷══◉

"What's the big fucking deal?" Dawn argued. "We're talking about one cop, a crooked-ass cop at that."

"I heard you the first time," Anthony replied. "Honestly, I'm just trying to figure out where all this is coming from."

Though she was an expert at acting tough, Dawn had the weight of the world on her shoulders. "Maybe I'm tired, Ant," she sighed. "Aren't you tired of all this? All the bullshit? We're always the victim, and I'm sick of it."

"We're only victims of our own choices. And you can't come back from killing…"

Dawn retreated to the solitude of her thoughts, the place where scars were hidden. For most of her life, she had been the victim of lustful and violent men, objectified and targeted by their demented desires. She had witnessed the evils of those with power, the corroded underbelly of human society, and it was enough to make her physically ill.

Anthony related to her frustration, more than anyone could. However, before he could conjure the words, he noticed a squad car creeping up the street, and a dreadful sensation instantly washed over him. Seeing the horror in his expression, Dawn slowly turned around, and her stomach dropped as the vehicle parked on the curb. With the engine still running, the driver's side door flew open, and a uniformed officer stepped out with a sinister grin. He was menacingly tall with soulless eyes, and approached them with his fingers tickling the handle of his pistol.

"Is that Anthony?" he grinned, spitting on the sidewalk. "Holy shit, I knew it was you. Imagine my surprise. Of all the alley's in all the world. What're the odds?"

Known as Officer Bennett, he was unanimously hated by all. His partner, Officer Hanson, exited the car with an evil glare, and stood nearby with savage intentions. Dawn huddled behind Anthony, too nervous to speak, while Bennet approached them with his chest out.

"How's the hand?" he taunted.

Anthony nervously clutched at his cast, recalling their last meeting. "Nothing I can't handle," he mumbled.

"An optimist; I admire that," said Bennett, glaring at Dawn with a cruel smile. "Tell me. What's a pretty girl like you doing with a piece of shit like this?"

She could smell the liquor fuming from his pores, and squeezed Anthony's arm with her mouth pinched shut. Bennett waited for a response, then crossed his arms in disapproval.

"It's not nice to ignore someone when they're talking to you."

"Look, we don't want any trouble," Anthony urged. "We were just leaving."

"But you'll miss the party," Bennett winked. "Hands on the wall. You know the drill."

"We haven't done anything," Dawn protested.

"Hands on the wall!" Bennett repeated.

Reluctantly, Dawn and Anthony placed their palms against the cold exterior of an adjacent building. Hanson chuckled in the background as Bennett conducted a rather invasive frisk, aggressively groping Anthony in his most sensitive areas and private parts.

"You really like your job, don't you?" Anthony griped.

"You have no idea," Bennett snarled in his ear.

As Dawn waited in limbo, she suddenly remembered the switchblade in her pocket. Bennett moved behind her with a perverted smirk, and the stench of alcohol was overwhelming. He slowly navigated his clammy hands up her dress, making her skin crawl, but she refused to be a victim twice in one night.

"Get the fuck off me!" she screamed, pulling away from his touch.

Without hesitation, he pushed her recklessly against the wall, slamming her head on the bricks. She fell awkwardly to the pavement, and a single thread of blood trickled from her left eyebrow.

"Don't be stupid!" Bennett hollered.

"What the hell's wrong with you?" Anthony yelled, jumping in his face.

In a flash, Bennett subdued him with a deadly chokehold. "Boy, you must be crazy!" he laughed.

Anthony clenched his teeth, struggling to breathe. "Please," he choked.

"Don't worry, I'll take good care of her," Bennett hissed. "All she needs is some tough love."

He punched Anthony in the kidney, buckling him to his knees, then struck him in the jaw for good measure. Watching with wide eyes, Dawn became blinded by rage. She pulled out the switchblade, then bolted toward the crooked officer with blood in her eye. With his back still turned, she shoved the knife directly in his right buttock, twisting the carbon steel. Bennett howled in agony, then backhanded her across the mouth, returning her to the curb.

"Stupid bitch!" he shouted. "What the fuck! You stabbed me in the ass!"

Clutching the pearled handle, he yelped as he firmly yanked the knife from his flesh, then angrily tossed it aside. While Hanson chuckled in amusement, Dawn remained on the sidewalk, frozen in a state of shock. Anthony was still prostrated on the ground, and their lamented eyes connected in desperation. She was right: they were always the victim, and the bitter truth was enough to ignite an invisible fire from within.

"Hey, Bennett," he coughed. "…Go fuck yourself."

The irritated officer faced him in disbelief. "Has everyone lost their fucking mind tonight?" he snarled.

Breathing heavily, Anthony gradually stood to his feet. "Better yet, how about you and your partner go fuck each other," he added.

Bennett slightly tilted his head, as if somewhat impressed. "Now ain't this some shit," he pointed. "Do I have to break your other hand?"

Without another word, he threw a swift jab, and Anthony stumbled backward to the concrete, his mouth full of blood. After he fell, Bennett kicked him hard in the gut, removing every molecule of air from his lungs. Lusting for destruction, the merciless officer unleashed a powerful series of ruthless combinations, pummeling his prey into the pavement.

"Stop it!" Dawn screamed. "You fucking psycho! You're gonna kill him!"

Ignoring her cries, Bennett continued his frenzy of savagery, indulging in his own deviltry. His knuckles were bloodied and enflamed as he dauntingly raised his fist, excited for another round. However, before he could deliver, someone abruptly seized him by the wrist. He furiously turned around, expecting to see his partner, only to be greeted by a wild-haired man in cowboy boots.

"Howdy," Dirt grunted, smoking a cigarette.

Struggling to free his arm, Bennett was surprised by his abnormally strong grip. "What the fuck!" he blurted.

Venting clouds of smoke, Dirt eventually relinquished his hold, giving Bennett a chance to reach for his sidearm. However, the cop quickly discovered his pistol was missing from its holster. As Dirt flicked his cigarette to the curb, he raised the officer's weapon with a playful grin. The lawman was absolutely dumbfounded, and his nostrils flared as Dirt quickly disassembled the nine-millimeter, sprinkling the metallic pieces atop the asphalt.

Meanwhile, Dawn was suspended in absolute awe, incapable of processing the sequence.

"Hanson, get your ass over here!" Bennett yelled nervously.

"Who?" Dirt shrugged. "You mean this guy?" He casually stepped aside, and the officer was startled to see his partner slumped awkwardly in the gutter.

"Oh my God!" Bennett exclaimed with wide eyes.

"We should probably let him rest," Dirt suggested. "I think he's done for the night."

"You're dead, motherfucker!" the cop shouted. He boldly swung at Dirt with the intensity of a prizefighter.

Nevertheless, Dirt saw it coming from a mile away, and instinctively caught his fist with both hands. With an iron grasp, he broke Bennett's index and pinky finger simultaneously, then rotated his wrist until it snapped. Then, Dirt used his forearm like a sledgehammer, and quickly struck the officer's elbow, breaking the joint. Finally, before releasing his grip, he dislocated the cop's shoulder in one smooth motion. Bennett dropped to his knees in pain, examining his mangled arm.

"Fuck!" he whimpered.

Dirt adjusted his collar in the wind. "That's the problem with this town," he sighed. "All the cops want to be gangsters."

He lifted Bennett to his feet, then flung him effortlessly against his own patrol car. The impact cracked the side window, and the officer collapsed to the curb, absolutely stunned. He frantically crawled across the blacktop, desperate to escape. Because the driver's side door was still open, he latched onto the front seat with his good arm, then tried pulling himself inside the car. However, Dirt viciously kicked the door closed, shattering his humerus bone.

Although Dawn winced at the sight, she enjoyed seeing the cop squirm with two worthless limbs. As Bennett squealed in the night, Dirt loomed over him like death itself, then violently stomped on his head, stamping the street with his skull. The screaming instantly stopped, and the faint horn of a distant train lingered ominously in the breeze. Dirt turned away from the bloody mess, then wiped his boot across a patch of dead grass, leaving a stain of red remains.

Dawn was still lying on the ground, her mind blown by the entire ordeal. She was lost in a frightful wonder, frozen with fear and admiration. Dirt calmly approached her, then politely held out his hand, though she was hesitant to accept it.

"You're safe now," he assured her.

Judging by his tone and demeanor, she knew he was a Soldier. She cautiously took his hand, then pulled herself to her feet.

"I don't know what just happened," she uttered, wiping the blood from her mouth. "But that was some of the craziest shit I've ever seen. And I've seen a lot of shit."

"Thank you," he smirked. "It's what I do."

Anthony had been unconscious during the melee. Fortunately, he was still breathing, though his face had an uncanny resemblance to roadkill. He eventually opened his swollen eyes, then rolled onto his back with a painful groan. Staring at a cherry moon, his hazy vision was suddenly eclipsed by a reflective pair of sunglasses.

"Top of the morning, brother," Dirt grinned, offering his hand.

Stuck in a stupor, Anthony studied his manner with extreme apprehension. "Who the hell are you?" he uttered.

"A friend."

Slightly tentative, Anthony cautiously reached out, and Dirt gladly helped him off the pavement. The teenager staggered to his feet, locked in a daze, then leaned against the wall with his ears ringing.

"What the fuck happened?" he grumbled, swallowing blood.

Dirt placed a cigarette between his lips, then casually lit the tip on fire. "You're alive, brother," he told him. "And that ain't bad for a bad day."

Nearby, Dawn was quietly standing over the mess that was once Officer Bennett. After being attacked twice in one night, her mind was an emotional collage, and everything was a blur. She was virtually on another planet. Anthony looked at her as the cool air danced around them, then meekly limped toward her with a burdened spirit.

"You okay?" he asked, rubbing his jawbone.

"I think so," she mumbled. "What about you?"

Anthony stood beside her, surveying the debilitated officers hugging the concrete. "Nothing I can't handle."

Dirt exhaled another smoke cloud as he studied their temperament. "If you ask me, you both look a little stressed out," he said, expressing his concern. "And full disclosure, I'm pretty sure one of you needs medical attention."

Before Anthony could reply, Dawn rested her head against his shoulder, and he held her close, embracing her in the light of the aftermath. "I think we'll be alright," he affirmed. "... We owe you one. I don't know what would've happened if you hadn't showed up."

"I wouldn't think about it too much," Dirt smiled.

Satisfied with the outcome, he nonchalantly walked to the police car, reached above the rearview mirror, and snatched the wires from the video control module. Then, inspecting the engine, he quickly ripped off a tracking device connected to the battery. After tossing the broken pieces aside, he finally sat behind the wheel with a smug expression. The radio system was flashing with mindless chatter, the dashboard was littered with coffee-stained paperwork, and a crinkled bag of glazed doughnuts was laying in the passenger seat.

Dawn watched in amazement, enamored by his fearlessness. "Are you for real right now?"

"I'm sick of walking," said Dirt, closing the door. "You two need a ride somewhere?"

Anthony quickly declined, waiving his hands in refusal. "Hell no," he answered. "I've had enough excitement for one night."

Dirt chuckled to himself as he revved the engine. "It's just another Saturday night for me," he shrugged.

He shifted the gear in reverse, then slowly backed off the curb into the empty street. "Listen," he continued, talking out the window. "I'm not trying to preach to you, but you need to do a better job of looking out for each other. They use kids like you for target practice, or worse. It's nothing to them. But at least you stood up for yourselves, and that's important. Don't ever lose that. Just try ducking next time." He gave an offhand salute, then stepped on the gas without saying another word. The tires screeched as he accelerated up the block, vanishing into the void of a dark metropolis.

Dawn looked down at the bodies one last time, then somberly went to retrieve Red's switchblade by the dumpster. Tonight, the Soldiers had done more for her than anyone ever could, and despite the media's malicious propaganda, she considered them true heroes.

"I can't believe you stabbed Bennett in the ass," said Anthony, still woozy.

"I can't believe you told him to go fuck himself," she voiced. "That was pretty cool."

"Really?"

"Absolutely."

Anthony was beaming as they cautiously made their way off the street corner, leaving the incapacitated officers for the elements. Life was a nightmare, but at least they had each other. Away from the traumatic scene, they ventured deeper into the concrete abyss, searching for anyplace elsewhere. "I'm pretty sure that guy was drunk," he muttered, referring to their mysterious savior.

CHAPTER EIGHT

Broken Mirrors

Within the putrid shell of a deteriorated building, two Soldiers were ascending a decaying stairwell, making their way toward the rooftop. As they rounded another sinking platform, the wooden floorboards warped and groaned beneath their feet. Many of the stairs were missing, and large portions of the handrail were absent, forcing them to hug the wall on multiple occasions to move forward. Skipping over a small gap, Numbers was enjoying a thin cigar, carrying a plastic container full of blue liquid.

"Do you have to smoke around that shit?" Horse complained, pointing a flashlight. "At least let me carry it."

"Man, let me do me," he sighed, blowing out smoke. "You gotta relax sometimes. Anyway, like I was saying, there's this game called *Killing People Fast*, where you get points based on how fast you kill people. It's crazy as fuck. I was playing it this morning."

"What kind of shit is that?" Horse questioned. "That's too unrealistic. You don't get points for killing people. You get the needle."

"But it's not supposed to be realistic. It's a form of escapism. Kind of like this other game called *Stealing People's Shit*, where all you do is break into people's houses and steal shit. It's made by the same company. I can't front, it gets old after a few rounds."

Horse ducked beneath a twisted steel beam. "That sounds stupid as hell," he argued. "If someone breaks into my house, the only round getting old is the one I put in his head."

Numbers laughed aloud as they reached the top landing. "Man, you're a trip," he chuckled. "You don't like video games, you don't watch movies, you don't listen to music, you don't drink...you're like a goddamn alien. Don't you have any hobbies or something?"

Horse pondered the question while swatting at a cloud of gnats in his path. "Soap carving," he said offhandedly. "It relaxes me."

After contemplating his reply, Numbers simply shook his head, amused and amazed. "I honestly don't know what the hell that is," he admitted.

At the top landing, moths clustered around the faded light of an exit sign, barely hanging above a rusted green door. Horse pressed against the panic bar, and the hinges creaked as they stepped outside, greeted by the cardinal moon. Soft winds gently shifted the clouds, revealing small assemblies of stars fixated in the tranquility of night. Red was standing peacefully at the edge, staring at a dark horizon, and all was ominously calm atop the ten-story structure.

They were at the epicenter of the Southland Quake, a sector of town where few dared to venture, considering it was a ten-mile radius of absolute devastation. Skeleton frames from shattered superstructures towered like metal monuments over ravaged streets, yielding phantoms and sinuous shadows that struck fear in the hearts of men. Piles of bricks and stones from torn skyscrapers cluttered the roads, while narrow avenues were congested with mangled lamp posts and mutilated cars covered in grime. These were relics of another time, ancient remnants of an era buried in the ashes of archaic ruins.

In the quiet solitudes of his mind, Red bitterly recalled that fateful morning. He remembered the streets tearing apart like fragments of brittle paper, and entire buildings crumbling to dust. Underground pipes exploded, spreading fires and floods simultaneously across the city. People were bathing in ashes, screaming with loved ones dying in their arms. There were no disaster-relief groups or celebrity fundraisers, no infomercials or inspirational pop songs. Only empty lip service from Mayor Durnum, vowing to rebuild a better and more viable South Los Angeles.

"You know, history's full of traitors," Red uttered, surveying the lifeless buildings. "Maybe it's the nature of man. Ever since Kane killed Able."

Slumped beside him was none other than Victor, Tree's most elite and trusted bodyguard, gagged and bounded to a wooden chair. He was sitting inches from the ledge, drenched in his own sweat, with horrific bruises and ghastly cuts covering his body. He had been tortured senseless and beaten beyond recognition. With his mouth taped shut, and a large knife planted in his quadriceps, he was waiting at death's door, wishing for it all to end.

"Smells like he pissed himself," Horse griped, leaning against a nearby column.

Numbers set the plastic container down by a parapet wall, then glared at their captive with little satisfaction. "He definitely pissed himself," he scowled.

Victor's cries were muffled as Red yanked the knife from his leg. "Then let's begin," Red nodded, ripping away the duct tape.

After a layer of skin was frayed from his lips, Victor lowered his head with a broken spirit. "Fuck you," he drooled. "Just kill me already."

"Don't spoil it for me, Vic," Red told him.

"You're wasting your time. I don't know shit."

"Oh, I doubt that," said Red, pointing his knife. "See, I got eyes and ears everywhere. Every block; every corner. I'm damn near omnipresent."

"Is that a fact?" Victor mumbled.

"That's why we're here," Red asserted. "I never liked you, Vic. To be honest, no one did. But there was something about you that I couldn't quite put my finger on. So, after what happened to Tree, I made sure someone was always watching you."

Victor was blinded by the blood in his eyes. "Kiss my ass," he said.

Red responded by striking him in the mouth, causing his head to drop below his shoulders. "As I was saying," Red resumed, rubbing his knuckles. "I know all about your little excursions, meeting up with your mystery woman. At first, I assumed it was your wife, or your girlfriend. But that never made sense to me, because nobody likes you. So, I put eyes on her. Come to find out, she's working for the FBI. Ain't that some shit? Agent Silvia Vicente, or some shit like that.

Imagine my surprise. I always knew Tree was set up, but I should've known you had a hand in it."

After spitting out a tooth, Victor tilted his head back with a bloody smile. "You might as well go 'head and kill me," he chuckled. "None of this even matters anymore; you're already fucked."

Numbers was feeling anxious. "I say we start cutting off body parts," he earnestly suggested. "Then we could force feed him pieces of himself."

"That's them video games talking," said Horse, sounding like a disapproving parent.

Red could feel the ice running through his veins. "What's the word, Vic?" he questioned. "You an agent? Informant? Inquiring minds want to know."

"You don't get it," said Victor. "You're so fucking worried about what I am, but I'm just a ghost. I'm nobody. I'm a fucking pawn…"

"Do I look worried?" Red countered.

"Maybe not," Victor admitted. "But you should be. I'm not the only pawn in this game…"

Narrowing his eyes, Red folded his arms, maintaining his disposition as the wind rushed over peaks and valleys of a desolate metropolis. "Is that supposed to mean something?" he asked coldly.

"Fuck this!" Numbers expressed. "This bitch is stalling! We already know he's guilty!"

"You don't know shit," Victor insisted. "Everything you think you know, is a lie. You think you're out here fighting the good fight? You think you'll change anything? Please. You're more delirious than I thought."

While Horse and Numbers exchanged irritable expressions, Red picked up the plastic container with a heavy sigh. "This is the part when I threaten someone close to you," he said ominously. "But we both know you're all alone in this. No one to care about, and no one that cares about you. Shit, Tree was the only one who ever gave a damn about your sorry ass, and he paid the price for it." He twisted off the cap, then showered Victor with the strange blue liquid. The icy substance was like an electric shock to his senses, causing him to recoil from the freezing elixir.

"What's the matter?" Numbers grinned. "Too cold? Try to relax. It's just something Bunchy brewed up for us. He's good at things like this. Smells like laundry detergent, don't it?"

"What the fuck is this shit?" Victor gagged.

"Not sure," Red confessed, pouring the last drop. "But it's highly flammable."

"Extremely," Horse added. "You'll light up like fireworks."

The prospect of being burned alive was something Victor had failed to consider, and as the pungent mixture flooded his nose, he imagined himself choking on the fumes of his own flesh.

"You don't know how to act, Vic," Red scolded. "That's not healthy."

"Wait a fucking minute!" Victor coughed. "You're out of your goddamn mind!"

"Don't tell me you're afraid of a little fire," Numbers taunted, playing with his lighter. "What happened to all that tough talk? Ain't this what you wanted?"

"I never wanted any of this shit!" Victor declared. "I already told you! I'm nobody! I'm at the bottom of the food chain!"

"Then who's at the top?" Red demanded. "Who's pulling the strings? Tell me, and I promise we can make this quick."

"You're insane!" Victor shouted, shaking nervously.

"And you're a dead man," Red glared. "So, we can do this JFK style, or we can get medieval. The choice is yours."

Victor clenched his fists, then tried not to panic as he sat helplessly in limbo. He was at the threshold of oblivion, face to face with his own mortality, and it made him realize the futility of his own existence. Between the seconds, his entire life flashed before his eyes, and he could see it was void of any true meaning. His reality was nothing more than following orders, with nothing to show for it but a series of painful regrets. He took a deep breath, then slowly exhaled as he settled into his plight. He was unable to fight it, because the truth was all around him. He was too insignificant to be saved. He was only a puppet, with absolutely nothing to lose and nothing to gain. It was too late for him now, and there would be no redemption.

"Fuck it, burn him," Red ordered, breaking the silence.

"Okay, okay!" Victor blurted, shivering in his seat. "I'll tell you; I'll tell you everything..."

Red pulled out a pack of menthol cigarettes. "You're smarter than you look," he smiled, placing one between his lips.

Victor tilted his head back in defeat, then hesitated before he spoke. "I *was* working for the government," he admitted, sighing dismally. "But it's a bit more complicated than that."

Red calmly lit his cigarette. "What's so complicated?" he shrugged, blowing smoke in Victor's face. "Tree was a powerful man. People loved him, and he was fearless, making him a threat. So, they assassinated him, and you helped orchestrate it. Tell me I'm lying."

"You really *are* clueless," Victor chuckled. "The man you knew as Tree Newman doesn't even exist. He never did. His real name was Jeremy Barnes."

This ominous telling was followed by an awkward silence, as if the heavens and earth stood still. Horse and Numbers were both somewhat puzzled, while Red simply raised an eyebrow as he quietly smoked his cigarette.

Feeling the tension in the air, Victor decided best to proceed with caution. "Jeremy was an asset for the Agency," he explained. "He was a sleeper agent."

"Is this motherfucker serious?" Numbers frowned.

"You wanted the truth," Victor grumbled. "I told you it's complicated…"

"Smells like bullshit to me," said Horse.

"Why the hell would I lie now?" Victor spat. "Look at me…I'm already dead. There's no fucking point…"

"He ain't lying about that," Horse shrugged.

Standing quietly at the ledge, Red was deep in his thoughts, high above a city of darkness. Over the past year, he had proven to be an elite strategist, a methodical mastermind, and his weapon of choice was always information. "I want to know everything," he eventually said.

"Then you should listen very carefully," Victor nodded. "Jeremy Barnes was programmed to start a terrorist cell on domestic soil. Period. That's what this is; that's why you're here. It's all part of the program. The SRS is nothing more than a black op for the CIA. One of many, I'm afraid…"

Numbers threw his arms up in dissent. "Why are we still listening to this?" he protested.

"I'm starting to wonder myself," Red agreed. "Come on, Vic. You can't honestly expect us to believe that shit. Because that would be an insult to our intelligence."

"It doesn't matter what you believe," Victor replied. "Just think for a second. It's about power, influence, it's about controlling both sides of the board. The bombings, the shootings, the riots. They're all coordinated events. Everything's manipulated, even the weather..."

"What the hell are you babbling about?" Red groaned.

"The country's changing, Red," Victor explained. "It's a new world out there, and the government's willing to do whatever it takes to maintain control, even attack its own citizens. Think about it. Fear is the only thing keeping this shit together. When people are afraid, they become desperate... they lose hope. Cause enough chaos, and people will beg for guidance, protection; they'll beg for law and order. It's as simple as that."

Red exhaled a large cloud of nicotine. "Then what happened?" he mocked. "If this is all part of some elaborate government plot, why kill Tree? Or better yet, why is your dumb ass tied to a chair? Guess the plan ain't going so well, huh?"

"On the contrary," Victor boasted. "The plan's flawless. They have cells all over the country. But poor Jeremy was a special case. He was smart and charismatic, but he had no idea he was being controlled. Ever heard of MK Ultra? Well, that's preschool shit compared to what they do now. I was supposed to monitor his progress. But the psyche can only take so much before it cracks, and his brain started rejecting the program..."

"Why's he still talking?" Numbers sneered.

Victor lowered his head in reverence. "He figured it out in the end," he mumbled. "Poor bastard. He was about to expose everything, so the Agency pulled the plug. Killed the whole operation. That means every person, place, or thing connected to the Soldiers has to go. That's how it works. As for me, I guess I know too much for my own good."

"A victim of circumstance," Red scoffed.

"Aren't we all? Jeremy recruited *you*, didn't he? I bet that wasn't too difficult. Wasn't your father killed by a cop? When you were a kid, they shot him in his own house, right? Yeah, I wonder where that puts *you* in this equation. You're just another pawn, Red. You always have been. Just like Jeremy. Just like *me*."

Rolling the cigarette between his fingers, Red smiled politely, then calmly stepped away. When he was just eight years old, a burglar foolishly invaded his home. His father, being an honorable man, defended his family with three shots from his Ruger, while his mother, being a Christian woman, promptly called the police to make a report. However, once the officers arrived, they murdered his father in cold blood, falsely identifying him as the invader. Afterward, his mother was utterly heartbroken, beyond devastated, and eventually sent to a mental institution, where she later committed suicide.

Thus, Red's devotion to the Soldiers was unbreakable. After turning toward his comrades, he slid his thumb horizontally across his throat, signaling the inevitable. They gestured their acknowledgment, then stepped back in anticipation.

"I must say, this has all been very enlightening," Red announced. "And who knows? Maybe we're all pawns; maybe this is all a game. Maybe there's some malevolent force out there, controlling everything like some mystery God in the sky. But guess what? I don't give a fuck, because at least I'm not you."

He flicked his cigarette in the air, and Victor was horrified as it landed softly in his lap, instantly igniting the blue liquid. In a flash, a massive fireball erupted, causing Red and his men to jump backward as colorful sparks shot in every direction. Engulfed in a bright cloud of scorching heat, Victor let out an earth-shattering scream, helpless as his flesh carbonized and scattered in a dazzling whirlwind of florescent embers.

Horse shielded his face from the giant flames. "Holy shit!" he shouted.

Reacting instinctively, Red swiftly kicked the human bonfire in the chest, launching him off the roof, and Victor was still howling as he fell a hundred feet to a dismal death. Landing in the murky abyss, his body splattered against the sidewalk, painting the pavement with his roasted entrails.

As silence gradually descended, Red slowly approached the smoky ledge, then looked down at a fiery corpse in a lagoon of darkness. "Damn."

Numbers was absolutely stunned. "What the hell was that!" he exclaimed. "We almost burned up with the motherfucker!"

"Maybe we should go back to using kerosene," Horse noted.

"No shit," said Numbers, brushing charred remains off his cargo vest. "Is it me, or does it still smell like laundry detergent?"

Posted at the edge of the world, Red was surrounded by currents of glowing cinders, twisting and curling in a radiant tapestry. After a brief meditation, he eventually turned around, then proudly marched toward the green door at the opposite end of the roof. "Let's get the fuck out of here," he ordered.

CHAPTER NINE

Scrap Metal

Sprawled across the cold surface of his office desk, Bunchy was fully detached from reality, staring at the formlessness of space. After ingesting a healthy dosage of Reaper Dust, his psyche was a collage of malice and dysphoria, an endless cycle of lamented afterthoughts. Clutching Samson's medallion, he slowly drifted away, falling deeper into his own personal purgatory.

"So, this is it, huh?" said a familiar voice.

Somewhere in the void between visions and dreams, he could see his cousin sitting peacefully in the corner, appearing healthy and young with a radiant glow. Overwhelmed with emotion, Bunchy remained perfectly still, questioning his own sanity.

"After everything we've sacrificed," Samson told him. "After everything we've lost."

Bunchy held his breath, tears swelling in his eyes. "It should be me instead of you," he said eventually. "...It should have been me."

"It wasn't your choice to make."

"But I could've done something," Bunchy argued.

"Like what?"

"Anything!" he sobbed. "Anything would've been better than watching you die!"

Samson leaned back with a serene demeanor. "Life is smoke," he grinned. "It always fades away."

"But you...you sacrificed yourself," Bunchy mumbled. "And I just watched it happen."

"It was out of your hands."

Bunchy shook his head as he turned away, stricken with sorrow. "You expect me to accept that?" he uttered.

"No. I expect you to live. Just live."

"How the hell do I do that?" Bunchy wept.

Samson slowly ascended to his feet. "Well, you can start by getting up," he smiled.

Without another word, he vanished in the same manner as he manifested, and Bunchy was alone once again. Suspended in a trance, he slowly opened his eyes, then lethargically sat in bewilderment, wiping the tears from his face. The experience was far too powerful to ignore. He carefully scanned the room, as if searching for an explanation, then stared solemnly at the empty chair nearby.

"You motherfucker," he thought aloud. "...Okay. I hear you."

With sweat pouring from his brow, he sorely propped himself on the edge of the desk, still woozy from the drugs and blood loss. While gathering his strength, he instinctively glanced at the security monitor, and his expression suddenly intensified. Staring at the dusty screen, he saw a team of heavily armed agents tinkering with the entrance of the bunker.

"Fucking beautiful," he grunted.

He struggled to his feet, but quickly lost his balance and fell painfully to the floor, ripping the stitches in his leg. "Get your shit together, old man," he scolded himself.

Knowing the door could open at any second, he scoured the archives of his mind, recalling every piece of equipment in his arsenal, then desperately crawled toward a crate full of various explosives.

⋄══

The air was cold within the dark and shattered ruins of Bunchy's Pawn Shop. The once beautiful and thriving emporium had become a collection of dead bodies and empty shell casings, a medley of blood and bullet holes. At the far end of the concrete burial ground, five agents in tactical gear were gathered by the staircase in anticipation. As one adjusted the night-vision settings on his rifle, he stared at the sea of numerous corpses, fearful of the same fate: his name was Roosevelt.

"I wish you'd hurry up," he griped. "Smells like shit in here."

He was talking to a man named Carter, who was kneeling by the stairs with a specialized gadget in his hands. Holding the silver contraption over the first tread, the miniature device was designed to bypass digital locks, yet time was needed to match the specific encryption.

"This would go a lot faster if you'd shut the fuck up," he sighed, watching the signal closely.

Suddenly, the small apparatus flashed a sequence of green numbers across the touchscreen, and a metallic noise rattled loudly from the wooden stairs. The team quickly ducked behind nearby shelves and broken display counters, ready with their weapons drawn. Poised in attack position, Roosevelt was locked and loaded, aiming his rifle in the darkness. He heard gears shifting in the walls, then the sound of air being released, before the stairwell gradually ascended like a drawbridge.

"Presto," Carter whispered.

Roosevelt nodded at him, then cautiously moved toward the entryway.

"Alright, assholes," he ordered. "On my six. And try not to die."

He warily stepped over the threshold, while his team followed tentatively behind. Creeping silently through a miniature hallway, they soon found themselves in a dimly lit chamber full of military weapons, tactical gear, and unidentified technological advancements. After noticing the medical supplies and bloody towels scattered across a table, Roosevelt signaled his men to stay alert as they quietly searched the area. As Carter surveyed the room with his rifle steady, ready to fire at anything that moved, he discovered small droplets of blood at the tail end of the bunker, and followed the trail down a dark aisle of various gun attachments. His adrenaline spiked with each step as he made his way toward a single row of tall metal cabinets.

Less than ten feet away, Bunchy was hiding in a weapons locker, patiently waiting for an opportunity to strike. Glaring through the vents, he was beyond the point of exhaustion, battling the pain surging throughout his body. It was strenuous enough to keep himself from passing out. However, after staring death in the face and kissing the hereafter, he planned to go out with a bang.

He was holding an improvised explosive device, packed with nail heads, broken razors, and other sharp bits of metal, as well as a generous amount of gunpowder. Needles were sticking out of the shell, and the frame was wrapped in paper glued to large shards of glass. Complete with a pull-ring fuse and five-second delay, it was a certified nail bomb. Tensely waiting, he watched Carter pass without being detected, then quietly opened the door.

Searching in the shadows, the agent was startled by two taps on the shoulder. He turned around, only to be stabbed brutally in the throat as the bomb impaled his jugular. Bunchy swiftly pulled out the ring, then shoved him to the floor before jumping back inside the storage locker. While holding the door shut, he hollered out to purposely alert the others, and the remaining agents rushed to the end of the chamber. They found Carter with his face on the ground, soaking in his own fluids. Horrified, they scrambled to his aide, and as they rolled him on his back, Roosevelt had just enough time to see the explosive spiked in his throat.

KABOOM!

Carter's head exploded in a cumulus cloud of scattered molecules, and fragments of shrapnel darted in every direction, dicing through the agents with ease. Bunchy was sheltered from the blast as dozens of nails punctured the storage locker, missing his face by mere inches. However, he was still holding the door shut, and a select few managed to pierce painfully through his left forearm. *"Ssshhhit!"* he hissed in torment.

He slowly pushed the locker open with a grunt, then collapsed on the floor with his arm still pinned to the door.

Breathing deeply through his teeth, saliva oozed from his mouth as thick strands of blood leaked from his flesh. It took everything he had to pry away from the six-inch nails, even more to keep himself from screaming. It was a slow process, and after enduring the excruciating ordeal, he remained slouched on the ground, clutching his new wounds.

The team of agents had been annihilated, butchered in a bombardment of jagged metals. Severed body parts were stapled to the walls, and the ceiling was dripping with blood as scarlet rivers flowed effortlessly across the ground. Admiring his own handiwork, Bunchy struggled to his feet, then painfully limped around the mangled corpses. Surprisingly, Roosevelt was still alive, fighting for every breath as he laid motionless by a steel closet. He was sprawled next to his rifle, the barrel wet with blood. He had stumps for hands, needles were protruding from his eyes, and his face had the resemblance of burnt shredded cheese.

"Help me," he croaked blindly. "Please..."

Bunchy stood over him like a tyrant, then calmly picked up the weapon. "I really wish you would've killed me," he uttered.

Holding the gun at point blank range, he angrily squeezed the trigger until the magazine was empty, dicing the agent into chunks of matter. After leaving nothing left to identify, he casually tossed the rifle aside, then staggered away with a scowl. He hobbled toward the front of the chamber, leaving red footprints as he approached the security monitor. He punched a few numbers on the keyboard with a bloody finger, initiating a countdown for a detonation sequence.

He slowly exited the bunker, then somberly leaned against a support beam to catch his breath. Back in the misty gloom of his shop, he mournfully lowered his head with his eyes closed, lost in the shambles of his life. Suddenly, he felt the dreadful sensation of being watched. He quickly retracted his pistol, aiming at a phantom in the darkness, then hesitated when he saw it was merely a homeless man standing amongst the wreckage.

"Damn, this place is fucked up," the man slurred, clearly intoxicated. "…Smells like shit, too."

"Get the fuck outta here!" Bunchy shouted.

"I was just leaving," the man grumbled, vacating through a giant hole in the wall.

Isolated once again, Bunchy lowered his gun in bewilderment. He staggered over blood puddles and brass casings, lost in a garden of ghosts, until stumbling upon Samson's body in the rubble. He wavered in lament, clutching at the medallion tucked under his shirt, and realized all he could do was move forward. He owed it to his cousin.

After wandering outside, he noticed the entire block was completely deserted. He took a moment to steady himself, then painfully walked toward a ragtop convertible parked at the corner. With the keys in his good hand, he opened the door and collapsed in the driver's seat, wondering if he was still dreaming. He turned on the engine, then stared blankly at the abandoned road in front of him.

"Nice work," said Samson, materializing in the rearview mirror. "So, what's next?"

"I don't know yet," he mumbled, shifting the gear into drive.

Samson was beaming proudly. "Just live, cuzzo," he said. "Just live…"

Shedding tears, Bunchy stepped on the accelerator without looking back. The bunker exploded behind him, igniting the pawn shop in a fiery burst of hot metal and concrete, shaking the ground as burning chunks of debris launched high into the air. Rolling black clouds of smoke cascaded toward the sky, and the entire building imploded upon itself, sinking dramatically into the earth, leaving a smoky pit of ashes and embers.

CHAPTER TEN

Heaven and Earth

The city was alive in the dark hours of the night, full of wondrous terrors and dangerous delights. Concrete landscapes blossomed in the crimson moonlight, birthing a playground for nocturnal creatures, both predator and prey. Every shadow was alive, every corner had a story, and the streets were always watching. In the ghost town of Maywood, Geronimo was walking behind Kali, still battling the effects of the Reaper Dust. His world was a distorted configuration of amorphous shapes and nebulous angles, plagued by shifting phantoms and supernatural visions.

"We're almost there," said Kali for the third time.

Phasing between dimensions, he could see rays of light emanating from her entire body, like an ocean of shooting stars. He looked up toward the heavens, and colorful rifts stretched across the firmament as a dark cloud bombarded his senses. Losing control, he buckled against a nearby wall, then began vomiting profusely on the pavement.

"What the hell?" Kali exclaimed, rushing to his side.

He signaled for her to stay back, his face in the gutter. "I'm good," he heaved, hurling once again.

"What the hell happened?"

"I'm good, really," he puked.

"This shit is crazy…"

After gathering his bearings, Geronimo spat on the ground, then slowly straitened his posture. "I feel better now," he groaned, wiping his mouth.

"What the hell's going on with you?" Kali demanded.

"It's nothing. Don't worry about me."

He started to walk away, but Kali placed her hand softly on his chest. "Why do you always do that?" she questioned him. "I get it, you're a tough guy. But maybe you should try talking instead of pushing me away. It's called 'communicating'…"

"Are you flirting with me?" he smirked.

Kali sucked her teeth as she turned around. "Remind me to find you a mint," she sighed, continuing forward.

A wild dog howled in the distance as he checked his breath, slightly embarrassed. Following behind her, they hiked over paved hills of broken streetlights and crooked palm trees, touring various alleyways and barren fields of gravel, until the buildings were few and far between. The duo eventually reached a single-track railway overrun by jagged trees, and crickets were singing from the underbrush. Guided solely by the light of the moon, the trail was covered by thickets of brittle twigs and dead leaves that crumbled beneath their boots.

"Alright," Geronimo voiced, breaking the silence. "You wanna talk, then let's talk. I think we should get the fuck out of LA; get as far away from this shit as possible. We'll go to the mountains, or the desert, or an island, or whatever. We can live off the land, maybe grow old together..."

Kali paused by a barb-wired fence. "Do you hear yourself?" she frowned. "You're talking about abandoning the Soldiers."

Approaching her innocently, Geronimo hesitated before he spoke. "Most of the Soldiers are either dead, or locked up in some underground prison. Face it, there is no SRS. Not anymore."

"How could you say something like that? What the hell would Tree think?"

"Tree's gone, that's my point. It's the end of the world, and it's just us out here. Maybe it's time we start looking out for ourselves."

His words struck a nerve, and she was unable to hide her discontent. "If you wanna run, then be my guest," she voiced. "But this is bigger than us. Look around you. No matter where you go, no matter what you do, you'll always be a target. You'll always be hunted. You can't run from that; you can't hide from the truth. Tree understood that. Why can't you?"

"Please. This ain't rocket science," he argued. "This is war. And you wanna know how it ends? It doesn't. It just keeps going, and going...and nobody ever wins."

Kali glared at him intensely, looking through the windows of his soul. "Nobody lives forever, either," she countered. "If it's important enough, you should be willing to die for it."

Ending the conversation, she turned away and continued along the rusted track.

"Great talk," Geronimo mumbled.

After passing numerous caution signs, the single-track line guided them over a short service bridge, and they emerged at the threshold of an abandoned trainyard. Concrete towers rose over dismantled flangeways, and broken fragments of construction materials were scattered among the grounds. The entire area was on the verge of being reclaimed by mother nature. Roots of nearby trees had broken through the foundation, and wild plants were growing beneath the wheels of old locomotives. Crows were picking at shrubs sprouting from the cracks in the pavement, while a black cat observed from atop a graffiti-covered freight container.

As they made their way down a graveled aisle of dusty box cars, Geronimo had a strong feeling they were being followed, and discretely retracted his pistols. "Something ain't right," he uttered.

Kali rolled her eyes as she walked ahead. "What is it now?" she sighed.

Suddenly, a dozen men armed with small caliber weapons appeared on top of two parallel trains, surrounding them from above.

"Oh shit!" she blurted, aiming her rifle in every direction.

"Drop it!" demanded a raspy voice, piercing through the darkness.

Geronimo was shuffling between targets. "You first!" he yelled.

"I said drop your weapons!" the voice commanded.

With her right index ready on the trigger, Kali raised her left hand as a gesture of peace.

"Hold on, this is all just a misunderstanding!" she told them. "My name's Kali! I'm friends with Zora! We can clear this up right now if someone could just go get her!"

A woman wearing a brown duster jacket stepped forward from the shadows. Smoking a cigarillo, she had long gray dreadlocks and a prominent scar over her cheek bone. She sternly approached them, then a smile gradually sketched itself across her face.

"Kali!" she declared. "Holy shit, I didn't know it was you!"

Relieved, Kali lowered her rifle with a tired smirk, and the two embraced like long-lost relatives.

"Sorry about that," Zora explained. "Pigs been harassing us all month; we're a bit edgy. Goddamn Vikings. I'm telling you, they're like the fucking Nazis, but shittier. Way shittier."

Geronimo was still undecided, having never encountered this woman in his life. "Is this how you treat all your guests?" he scowled, still aiming his pistols.

"No offense, but have you seen yourself?" Zora shrugged. "You look like a pissed-off Rambo."

"It's okay, Moe," Kali insisted. "She's good people, I swear."

After much deliberation, Geronimo reluctantly holstered his guns, cursing to himself.

"Sorry, it's been a long night," Kali hinted to Zora. "That's why we need your help. And you know I wouldn't ask, unless it was serious. But we need food, water, and a car if that's possible…please."

Zora released a cloud of smoke, chuckling under her breath. "I figured this wasn't a social call," she smiled. "Well, so much for pleasantries."

After signaling the men to fall back, she escorted the duo through a labyrinth of vandalized trains, taking them deeper through the transit yard. Industrial chimney stacks stretched high toward a canopy of infinite night, and the air was filled with the ambiance of humming insects and russtling rodents.

"It's fucked up what happened to Tree," she said sympathetically. "From what I could tell, he was a good man. A bit eccentric, but he had the right idea. Blowing up Bryson's house was some bold shit, though."

"Just fighting fire with fire," Kali replied.

"That's the only thing they understand," Zora acknowledged. "Imperialist bastards. They still think it's the fucking Crusades…"

Geronimo was silently enduring his vexations as they traversed the dark train yard.

"Hey, Rambo, what's in the bag?" Zora asked him.

"Laundry," he grunted.

"Looks heavy," she said, playing along. "Must be a lot of clothes."

"Yeah…I'm a fashion model," he told her.

It wasn't long before the trail opened, and they reached a massive clearing fenced off from the canal. Illuminated by the orange glow of burning waste bins, the landscape was filled with oxidized rigs and deteriorated buildings. Fields of barren tracks laced together seamlessly like the web of a spider, intersecting broken rods and steel platforms in a collection of decaying metal. However, despite these conditions, there were alpine tents and sleeping bags everywhere. Ripped bedsheets were draped over entryways of damaged boxcars, and various shopping carts were parked beside open freight containers. The once abandoned rail yard had been converted into a refugee camp, sheltering those from all walks of life. It was a sanctum for lost souls.

The atmosphere was lively and filled with chatter. Soul music was being played on an ancient stereo, and children were enjoying cheap firecrackers while adults lounged on withered furniture sets. Folks were smiling and laughing, grilling food and drinking beer, dueling cards and slamming dominoes. Geronimo was transfixed on a mother and son playing catch with a deflated football, reminding him of a childhood he never had. The young boy waved at him innocently, and he returned the gesture with subtlety.

"What is this place?" he awed.

"Nowhere, really," said Zora, somberly. "After the quake, a lot of us had nowhere to go. And when I tell you things were bad, trust and believe. Shit, the shit got so bad, people were eating the dead. It's hard to imagine…but not if you lived it. Anyway, a few of us found this little slice of heaven, and the rest is history. We have a generator, a purifier, and we grow our own food. We're surviving; I guess that's good enough for now."

"It's illegal to grow your own food now," Kali voiced.

"Of course it is," Zora scoffed. "It's also a felony to scratch your own ass!"

She ultimately led them to a large warehouse at the south end of the property. They followed her inside, and Geronimo was amazed to be on the ground floor of a vertical farm. Light-emitting diodes and metal-halide lamps were hanging above vast rows of raised garden beds, and wooden planters full of fresh produce were stacked next to large water tanks and filters.

"They'd probably throw me under the jail for this shit," Zora sighed, walking to the center of the greenhouse. "You'd think I was selling dope. Damn devils. They'll give you a hundred years over a fucking salad. Whatever, humanity's fucked. Am I right?"

Geronimo noticed a patch of marijuana plants growing nearby. "No doubt," he acknowledged, discretely plucking a few buds for himself.

"Anyway," Zora continued. "As you can see, we have plenty of food and water, so feel free to help yourself. And I can get a car for you. It might need a little work, but I can have it ready for you in a few hours. Until then, you can stay in one of our trailers out back. Mi casa, su casa. I would lend you my truck, but I know how you Soldiers like to drive…"

"Thanks, Z," Kali grinned in gratitude. "I owe you one."

"Oh, I'm afraid you do," Zora smiled. "Because it's gonna cost you."

"What?" Kali frowned. "Seriously?"

"Hey, vehicles are a luxury around here," Zora explained. "You know how it is. Something like that requires a trade."

Geronimo was leisurely examining a school of colorful fish in one of the tanks. "Everyone's a capitalist," he muttered to himself.

"We don't have anything to trade!" Kali argued.

"You sure about that? What about those guns?"

Alerted by her suggestion, Geronimo immediately turned around with a raised eyebrow. "What guns?" he bluffed.

"Cut the shit, Rambo," she chuckled. "You might be cute, but you ain't no fashion model. And I know damn well you're not carrying around your dirty-ass drawers. Look, it's no secret. You guys roll with heavy artillery, and my people need guns. It's as simple as that. Wheels for weapons. What do you say?"

Geronimo clearly had his reservations about the deal.

"Moe, give her the bag," Kali told him.

Though he wanted to protest, her hazel eyes begged him to comply, and it became obvious that her connection to this place was painfully strong. With a sorrowful expression, he let the bag sink to his feet, despite it going against his better judgment.

"Wonderful," Zora declared. "Your car should be ready in no time. Until then, make yourself at home. I'll be in my office if you need me."

Afterward, Kali and Geronimo were given a large bowl of fresh fruits and vegetables, then directed to a small cul-de-sac of cargo trailers not far from the vertical farm. As they walked along a distorted chain link fence, they were surrounded by giant wooden crates and iron beams sprouting from the gravel, and a strong scent of burnt rubber saturated the air. They were given access to a lone trailer at the end of the path. It had a kitchen area with a sink, a small bathroom with a functioning shower, and a brown convertible sofa bed.

Pleased with the furnishings, Kali sat on the couch, biting into a juicy strawberry. "This is kind of nice," she smiled, kicking off her boots. "It's almost better than your apartment."

"Must be the presidential suite," Geronimo griped, leaning against the door.

Kali put her rifle down by the armrest, then slowly took off her assault vest. "Don't be like that," she sighed, rubbing her neck.

"Like what?" he grumbled, staring out the window.

"Like *that*. Now sit down and eat something."

She could always tell when he was upset.

"I'm not hungry," he uttered, pulling a blunt from his pocket. "...I can't believe we gave up those guns."

"Consider it your good deed for the day," she voiced, mouthful of spinach. "They need them more than us."

"These days, a good deed can get you killed," he remarked, sparking the leaf on fire.

"We're still Soldiers, Moe. In case you forgot, we're supposed to be helping people."

Geronimo reclined against the kitchen sink, then exhaled a monumental cloud. "And how's that been working out?"

Kali gave him a dirty look, then stretched her legs out on the sofa. Moonlight was shining in through the window, and festivities from the camp could be heard in the distance. With her arms folded behind her head, she watched layers of smoke curl gently toward the ceiling, and gradually allowed herself to relax. Meanwhile, Geronimo was trying not to stare at her shapely physique, failing miserably.

"So, you and Zora seem pretty close," he said, flicking ashes in the sink. "You never mentioned her before."

"I'm sure there's a lot we don't know about each other," she sighed.

Born on a remote farm outside the city, Kali's upbringing was far from conventional. Abandoned by her mother as an infant, she was raised by her father, who was a hardcore survivalist, a doomsday enthusiast, and an overall unbalanced individual. While other children enjoyed childish games, she was learning unarmed combat techniques, or identifying plants with medicinal effects. Ultimately, the ATF raided their farm when she was fourteen, and her father was inevitably sent to prison.

"Z was there when our farm got raided," she explained. "That's how she got that scar. I think she used to date my dad. She looked out for me, but we kind of lost touch for a while. When I found out she was staying here, I wanted to help. I got to know some of the people, their families. Everyone's just trying to live. You know?"

Geronimo hit the blunt with a subtle smile, admiring her compassion. He took off his jacket and tactical vest, then sat on the floor by the couch, smoke pouring from his nostrils.

Kali shifted onto her side, twisting strands of hair around her finger.

"What about you?" she asked. "You never really talk about your life. Before the SR…"

As a youth, Geronimo was forced to grow up fast. His mother was a founding member of the Poor Righteous Army, a band of urban guerrillas eradicated from history. They were always on the run; always hiding from the law. Eventually, she was arrested for the murder of a state trooper. She managed to escape from prison, then fled the country, leaving him and his brother in the care of their grandfather. He was twelve years old the last time he saw her, and a day rarely passed without him recalling their moments together.

"There's nothing really to talk about," he murmured. "It was just me and my brother for a while. Living like outlaws."

Kali reached over and plucked the blunt from his fingertips, then softly inhaled the smoke. "What made you join the SRS?" she asked.

Geronimo scratched at his recent bullet wound, inspecting the bandage. "My brother," he confessed. "He's the one who convinced me to join. But with everything that was going on, he didn't have to try too hard. I probably would've joined anyway. What about you? Never mind, I already know the answer…"

"And what's that?"

"You're a good person," he insisted. "You like helping people. If you weren't doing this, you'd probably be a doctor somewhere, or something."

Slightly blushing, Kali was somewhat taken aback. "And what would you be?"

"Me? I'd probably be a poet."

Kali laughed to herself. "I heard you got kicked out the Marines," she coughed with a smile.

"You heard about that?" he chuckled. "Yeah, guess I wasn't too good at following orders. But in my defense, I was barely sixteen. I had to forge my own birth certificate to get in."

"Wait," she said sternly. "You were sixteen? That's crazy..."

"Maybe, but I wanted to be strong. Growing up, I knew my mom needed help...but I was too weak to help her. And when she left...I don't know. It made sense at the time."

The room was getting hazy as she listened intently, allured by the deep tone of his voice. She passed him the evaporating leaf, then sat up with her elbows against the armrest.

"I never knew that about you," she said.

"I'm sure there's a lot we don't know about each other," he mocked, rotating his shoulder.

Rolling her eyes, Kali situated herself behind him, then started gently massaging his back, rubbing out the knots in his muscles. "You can really be an asshole sometimes," she smirked.

Enchanted by her magic touch, he was instantly under a spell. "Now I know you're flirting with me," he said, closing his eyes. "...Listen, all that stuff I said earlier; you were right. Forget I mentioned it."

With a sigh, Kali slowly stood up, then seductively straddled his lap.

"But were you serious?" she asked, tracing a finger along his chest. "Would you really run away with me?"

Pleasantly surprised, Geronimo quickly extinguished the leaf, then placed his hands upon her well-rounded backside. "I like where this is going," he smiled, holding her close.

"Answer the question," she purred, gripping firmly with her thighs. "Were you serious?"

"I'm always serious."

"It's a nice thought," she whispered. "...And I like thinking about it."

"Me too."

She smiled as their hearts interlocked, and he responded by kissing her softly on the neck. She unbuckled his belt, nibbling gently on his ear. After he effortlessly unsnapped her bra, the two embraced in an intimate exchange of body and soul. With quiet sighs and heavy breaths, they merged together like heaven and earth, lost in a blissful world of passionate pleasure. A combination of light and shadow accentuated the rhythm of their hips, the motion of their lust. A tender kiss, a warm touch, a delicate caress. Swimming in a fantasy of shades and shapes, they explored each other's desires, escaping their harsh reality for an intimate moment of beauty.

CHAPTER ELEVEN

Wildfire

At the west end of the yard, a two-story railway tower was sloped against an elevated track. The outdoor staircase was corroded, and various broken windows were covered with blue tarp. On the second floor, inside the control room, Zora was sitting alone at a frayed operator's desk. The busted line board was stained with filth, and the traffic panel was cluttered with shredded dispatch equipment. Drinking from a bottle of gin, she was holding a faded picture from another life: a wrinkled photograph of her daughter and grandson smiling at the beach. It was undoubtedly her most prized possession, a reminder that she was happy once. Sadly, they were both swallowed by the quake, buried alive in the wreckage of their own home.

With trails of tears on her face, she somberly raised the bottle to her lips. Suddenly, her sanctum of melancholy was interrupted by the unmistakable noise of a low-flying helicopter. She almost choked as she sat upright, eyes wide with urgency. Rushing to the nearest window, she peeled back the wet tarp and looked toward the night sky. There it was: a black AH-1 Cobra circling overhead, shining a searchlight on the grounds below. Before she could react, she heard thunderous footsteps racing up the staircase. In a state of confusion, she turned around just in time to see a squad of federal agents burst through the door. They surrounded her with their weapons drawn, and she timidly put her hands in the air.

"You gotta be shitting me," she muttered, dropping the liquor bottle.

⊷═◎

As the two lovers entwined on the floor, a pale beam of light sailed above the trailer, illuminating the entire room.

"What was that?" Kali moaned.

Cursing to himself, Geronimo pushed her aside, then hurried toward the window with one hand holding up his pants. Staying beneath the frame, he could hear the rotary wings of a looming aircraft nearby. He cautiously peeked through the acrylic glass, then narrowed his eyes as the light swept past once again, confirming his paranoia.

"Motherfucker," he grumbled.

Feeling flushed, Kali was sitting topless on the couch. "What the hell's going on?" she asked.

Outside, federal agents were invading in full force, bringing terror to the once peaceful rail yard. Innocent civilians were brutalized and detained at gunpoint, as if they were animals abducted from the wild. While many screamed for help, others begged for mercy, yet very few dared to resist. Hearing the chaos, Geronimo immediately went for his gear.

"We gotta go," he announced, buckling his belt. "Party's over."

In a huff, Kali reluctantly fastened her bra. "What the fuck," she frowned.

The searchlight brightened up the room once more, causing Geronimo to duck down by the sink. He checked the magazines in his pistols, then quickly racked the slides.

"I told you it was one of those nights," he griped.

"Are you bragging right now?" she hissed, grabbing her rifle.

"I never brag."

As the copter soared overhead, he carefully cracked the door open for a better view, while she waited anxiously for his signal. A moment passed before the duo raced from the trailer, dodging the searchlight as they sprinted across the sandy gravel. Gusts of wind from the aircraft invoked cyclones of dust, forcing them to shield their eyes as they moved forward undetected. They took cover behind a moldy freight container near the main yard, and Kali shouldered her weapon as she peeked around the corner.

From their new vantage point, she could see a storm of heavily armed agents on a rampage, abusing their power without reticence. She watched as they ravaged through people and property, mercilessly thrashing anyone who posed a threat or challenged their authority. She witnessed an old man pleading for his life with blood smeared on his face, a weeping woman pinned to the ground with a forceful hand up her dress, and a child being carried away, kicking and screaming, with tears streaming down his cheeks. Amidst the mayhem, an agent was aiming his weapon at a family huddled by a chain link fence.

"Give me a reason!" he hollered. "I dare you!"

Kali could feel the rage coursing through her veins. As her senses heightened, her focus sharpened, and her trigger finger itched with anticipation. She was on the verge of succumbing to her emotions, ready to strike at that exact moment, until Geronimo swiftly grabbed her by the arm.

"They'll kill them if you start shooting," he told her.

She already had the agent in her crosshairs. "I can hit him from here," she gritted.

"No doubt. But are you willing to risk the lives of all these people?"

After a moment of contemplation, Kali lowered her weapon with a scowl on her face. The two began their trek through the turbulence, utilizing the shadows as camouflage. They navigated between empty box cars and broken cranes, averting rampant agents at every twist and turn. All around them, innocent men and women were being hog-tied and dehumanized. A teenager was being pummeled as they ducked behind a collection of steel barrels, a man was being dragged by his legs as they cornered a stack of large tires, and an elderly woman was thrown against a waste bin as they crept beside a row of giant crates. The maniacal agents were in a frenzy, firing powerful stun guns and loads of tear gas in every direction, resulting in waves of trampled bodies and tormented faces.

Kali was awestruck as they forged ahead through the turmoil, shrouded in ambiguity. They cut across the yard toward the west end, then crawled behind a line of concrete dividers near the control tower. She pointed her weapon over the small barrier, glaring through the scope. Scanning the confines of the tilted structure, she spotted a pair of agents guarding the perimeter.

Geronimo carefully peeked over the divider. "Tell me that's the exit," he said.

"Not exactly," Kali replied. "…It's Zora's office."

He ducked down with his shoulder against the barricade, shaking his head in frustration.

"What do you want me to do, Moe?" she argued, crouching beside him. "You want me to turn my back on everyone I care about? Sorry, but that ain't me. I can't leave her like this."

"I never said that. But you can't save everyone all the time. Look around you. Think about saving your own ass for once."

Determined to act, she angrily wrapped her shemagh scarf over her nose and mouth, then glared at him with fire in her eyes. Staring back into the blaze, he could feel her intensity, and realized he was wasting his breath. With a heavy sigh, he reluctantly pulled a black bandana from his pocket, then tied it around his face like a bandit.

"Fuck it," he grunted.

Kali repositioned her rifle atop the divider. "That's the spirit," she said, scoping the enemy.

⊷═◉

In front of the control tower, two heavily armed agents were guarding the doorway with an unwavering vigilance. However, one of them eventually stepped away from his post.

"Where the fuck are you going?" his partner barked.

"I gotta check on something," he replied offhandedly. "Is that okay with you?"

"Well, hurry the hell up! We got a job to do!"

"Yeah, yeah…"

Focused on pressing matters, he quickly ventured around the building. Once he hit the corner, he crossed a set of tracks before arriving at a slanted light pole. Beneath an orange glow, he relaxed his shoulders and loosened his pants, then exhaled as he relieved his bladder in the comfort of solitude.

"Fucking shit," he grumbled as urine splashed on his boots.

He rattled his leg in a huff, distracted by his own carelessness, then suddenly felt a slight chill on the back of his neck. He slowly turned around, and was instantly struck between the eyes by the stock of a heavy rifle. The powerful impact knocked him senseless, and his body bounced clumsily against the light pole before awkwardly capsizing in a puddle of his own piss. Standing over him, Kali shouldered her weapon, then signaled for Geronimo to advance. She watched him sprint silently across a field of shadows, moving like a huntsman with a vendetta.

The second agent was still by the entrance, clueless to the misfortune of his fallen comrade. He heard a whistle, then looked up in time to see Geronimo airborne with a flying knee strike, shattering his jaw, the velocity strong enough to send them both to the ground. Geronimo promptly punched him in the same spot for good measure, then rose to his feet with a groan. He casually brushed off his jacket, cursing to himself, while Kali waited patiently by the door.

"Looks like you lost a step," she whispered.

"You weren't saying that back at the trailer," he quipped.

She rolled her eyes, then cautiously entered the tower with her finger on the trigger. Her muscles were tense as she moved like a phantom, staying sharp and low to the ground. Geronimo followed her past the threshold, fully aware they were stepping in the hornet's nest. The first floor of the building was simply a green hallway, complete with holes in the plaster, and cracks in the distorted floorboards. Currents of air leaked through fragmented windows, stirring up cobwebs that draped over defective light fixtures. An ancient map of the facility was still hanging by the door, right above a lone fire extinguisher that had long been expired.

Moving in silence, they lurked toward a flight of stairs at the end of the corridor, where they could hear voices coming from the control room. Poised at the base of the steps, Geronimo stooped low with his back against the banister, while Kali ducked down with her weapon steadfast. She nodded at him with a potent glare, and he responded by calmly stretching his neck. After this subtle exchange, they slowly ascended the stairway, fearless and ready for combat.

Inside the control room, Zora was on her hands and knees, bleeding on the floor with a broken nose and busted lip. Surrounded by five ruthless agents, they circled her like vultures around a carcass, each with a thirst for blood and a desire to kill.

"Stop lying!" one of them yelled, punching her in the eye.

"Yeah, tell us the truth!" another added, kicking her in the ribs.

Bolder than the rest, one man leaned close to her ear. "You're boring us," he hissed. "I'm starting to wonder why we haven't killed you yet."

She responded by spitting blood in his face.

"You stupid bitch!" he hollered, striking her in the mouth multiple times.

It took three men to pull him back, while another stepped forth with a devilish grin. "Look, we already know what you're doing," he said calmly. "Brainwashing these poor people, training kids to be killers, recruiting them for the Soldiers. So, let's stop with the games, all this back and forth. If you help us, I promise it won't be as bad as you think. Instead of the needle, you'll be sent to a work camp. You'd be taken care of, you and your people."

Zora was struggling to catch her breath. "You guys have to be the dumbest motherfuckers on the planet," she heaved. "I already told you, I don't know shit about the Soldiers. This place is full of families. Old vets, disabled people; real Americans. But you wouldn't know anything about that, you fascist piece of shit…"

"She's funny," someone chuckled. "Let's get this over with. It'll be one less file to process."

"Exactly," another nodded. "I got more important shit to—"

Suddenly, a flurry of ammunition pierced his helmet and body armor, promptly ending his assertion in a grisly fashion. There were two men standing next to him, and their fate was just as bloody. Splashes of crimson splattered into a rose-colored mist, and all three bodies hit the floor like wet bags of trash. Kali quickly dashed into the room with her rifle still smoking, followed by Geronimo who immediately hurled his knife through the air, aiming with the accuracy of a smart missile. As one of the remaining agents fumbled with his weapon, the blade gruesomely impaled his esophagus like skewered food. He ineptly fell to his knees, clutching the handle with bloody hands, before dying with the pain frozen in his eyes.

Horrified by the sight, the last man standing was completely traumatized, though death was swiftly approaching him like a raging storm from the deep. Scrambling for survival, he desperately pulled Zora to her feet, then held her at gunpoint while simultaneously using her as a human shield.

"The fuck!" he shouted.

Kneeling by a busted control panel, Kali was ready to shoot. "Let her go!" she demanded.

The agent stepped back with his arm wrapped tightly around Zora's neck. "Back the fuck up!" he ordered.

Staying close to the wall, Geronimo drew his twin pistols from his double back holster. "Drop the gun," he growled, activating the laser sights.

Suspended in the line of fire, Zora was battling to breathe, powerless to defend herself. The agent was dragging her by the throat, shuffling backward toward the side door, desperate to reach the staircase outside.

"I said back the fuck up, damn it!" he stammered. "One more step, and I'll blast this bitch's head off! You hear me? I ain't playing with—"

His helmet suddenly flipped high into the air as his neck snapped back, and his lifeless body toppled awkwardly to the floor with his cranium split. He had inadvertently swayed too far to the left during his tirade, leaving enough space for Kali to shoot him twice through the nasal cavity. Zora barely had time to flinch as a bullet grazed her ear, and her heart was racing as she trembled uncontrollably, marinating in a man's blood.

Kali frantically ran to her side. "Z, you okay?" she asked, frantically examining her wounds.

Zora exhaled a sigh of relief, clutching her ear. "Damn," she chuckled nervously. "You two really know how to make an entrance..."

Geronimo holstered his pistols, then calmly retrieved his knife. "Let's just hope nobody heard us," he grumbled.

"I've never seen anything like that before," Zora smiled, still gathering her bearings. "I can't thank you enough."

"Don't thank us yet," he insisted. "We still need to get the hell out of here."

Kali nodded in agreement as she scanned out the window. "He's right, we gotta move," she affirmed. "Just keep your head low and stay close, alright? We'll make a run for the garage."

"We can take my truck," Zora suggested. "But what about my people? I can't just—"

BRAT-TAT-TAT-TAT-TAT!

Without warning, a wave of automatic gun fire struck her repeatedly in the chest. Chunks of meat and cotton fibers exploded from her torso, resulting in a spectacle of bloodshed. Kali impulsively recoiled behind a nearby switchboard, covering her head as the deafening discharge echoed throughout the room. Geronimo rolled behind the operator's desk, narrowly escaping the endless torrent of fire power. Shielding his face from aerial fragments, sparks and debris filled the air as high caliber rounds showered everything in range.

The shooter was surprisingly one of the agents, who had mistakenly been left for dead. Swallowing his own blood, he was sprawled on the floor with a high-powered rifle in his hands. Dozens of shell casings fluttered to the floor as he relentlessly squeezed the trigger, the barrel pulsating with light. He had enough strength to enact his vengeance, and a murderous glare shimmered in the black basins of his eyes. However, his weapon unexpectedly malfunctioned. Cursing to himself, he nervously attempted to clear the jam, until a shadow darted across the room. He suddenly felt a dark presence looming over him. When he looked up, the last thing he saw was the wrong end of Geronimo's Colt 1911.

After the execution, Geronimo turned around to see Kali on the verge of crying. She was kneeling next to Zora in a state of shock, quivering as she desperately tried saving her. Unfortunately, Zora was already numb to the world, her lifeless eyes staring past the void. Geronimo felt Kali's pain like a bayonet to the gut, but now was not the time to mourn. The agent's attack had alerted the entire camp, and he could hear the helicopter getting closer by the second. He ran to the window with his gun in hand, then pulled back the tarp for a glance outside. Just as he suspected, a horde of agents were advancing on the tower like wildfire.

CHAPTER TWELVE

Hornet's Nest

As the black helicopter hovered alongside the tower, Geronimo was crouched by the window, shielding his eyes from the searchlight. Knowing what was next, he turned around and called out to Kali, but she was lost somewhere between the here and the hereafter. She was consumed by her own disbelief, covered in blood with Zora's dead body in her arms.

Geronimo ran toward her at full speed. "Get down!" he hollered, throwing himself on top of her.

The moment his feet left the ground, the aircraft unleashed a wave of thirty-millimeter rounds, and a storm of heavy gunfire exploded through the walls with a blinding velocity, hitting harder than a megaton bomb. The aerial strike eradicated everything in range, flipping the control room upside down in an eruption of sparks and metal fragments, filling the air with clusters of smoky debris. The tower shook as Geronimo covered Kali like a blanket, and there was a moment in time when he feared the worst for them all. Scanning their surroundings, his mind scrambled for an exit strategy. Desperate for a miracle, he was astonished to see the answer to his prayers: the bag of weapons they traded away was laying by the staircase.

The aircraft eventually ceased fire, and they remained motionless on the floor as the searchlight coiled around them, probing for signs of their demise. After a short survey, the aircraft banked away from the tower, and the room became as silent as a cemetery. Laying in darkness, Geronimo could hear footsteps creeping up the stairs, and instantly rolled onto his shoulder with both pistols prepared to shoot.

"Get ready," he whispered to Kali.

As expected, three agents entered the room with their weapons drawn. Creeping through the shambles in a triangular formation, they stepped over bodies and bullet casings, using night-vision scopes as they searched every inch for remnants of the suspected terrorists. Blending with the shadows, Kali and Geronimo were hiding quietly under the operator's desk, staying low and out of sight. He could tell she was still in shock, because she had the demeanor of a lost child. Nonetheless, it only strengthened his resolve to protect her, and his muscles tightened as he cautiously peeked around the table, watching the enemy in darkness.

Utilizing stealth, he took her by the hand, and guided her silently to the opposite end of the room. Every step was a gamble as they delicately avoided detection, countering the agent's movements like a choreographed dance. Miraculously, they managed to reach the staircase without being seen. The men were clueless, and as Kali safely descended to the first floor, Geronimo was feeling more confident about their escape. With the precious bag of weapons just a few feet away, he reached out for the ragged shoulder strap, then carefully secured it around his neck.

"What the fuck?" he heard.

He looked across the room, and saw the agents were pointing their guns in his direction. Before he could even curse, they opened fire simultaneously. He recoiled as a reflex, and the storm of bullets diced everything around him, missing his frame by mere inches as he stumbled backward down the stairs in a cluster of dust and debris. Falling on the duffel bag, he tumbled over a few steps before his foot caught a rotted baluster, anchoring him to the handrail. While he was sprawled on his back, an agent ran to the top landing, and immediately flooded the narrow stairwell with a blizzard of ammunition. Geronimo raised his guns as he detached himself from the handrail, and started sliding backward on the duffel bag down to the first floor, desperately returning fire as bullets flew past his head. In a dramatic exchange of artillery, he managed to shoot the agent multiple times in the torso without getting hit.

He landed unscathed at the bottom of the stairs, heart racing with his fingers still on the triggers.

"Moe!" Kali screamed, rushing to his side.

"Behind you!" he yelled.

Five more agents were invading through the front entrance as she turned around, and her sorrow instantly transformed into unbridled rage. Without thinking, she fearlessly charged toward them with her rifle at the shoulder. She dropped to her knees, then slid across the dusty floor while frantically squeezing the trigger, leaving a bronze trail of bullet casings, killing them all in one sweep. Staying low to the ground, she pressed her back against the nearest wall, then rapidly switched magazines.

At the same time, two agents from the top floor were shooting their way downstairs. Geronimo narrowly escaped the cascade of bullets by doing an impressive barrel roll, then jumped to his feet before dashing to the end of the hallway, shooting blindly above his head as gunfire flared at his heels. Directly beneath the stairwell, Kali raised her rifle, squeezed the trigger, and columns of heat pierced the wooden steps, erupting in a geyser of hot metal. Both agents flopped lifeless to the bottom of the stairs while Geronimo ducked by the entryway to reload, cautiously peeking beyond the threshold.

Along with the copter circling overhead, a perimeter of trigger-happy agents behind a row of armored vehicles separated them from the rest of the world.

"Fuck this," he grumbled. He unzipped the duffel bag, then began scouring through a collection of strange and experimental firepower. He could hear shouts from the enemy as he quickly selected two thick pieces of carbine and attached them together. He loaded an unusual forty-millimeter shell in the chamber, then pointed the barrel outside.

"What the hell is that?" Kali whispered.

"Plan B," he grunted.

He squeezed the trigger, and a lone cylinder launched through the air at a surprising speed, leaving a vanishing trail of vapor. Spiraling toward one of the vehicles, it punctured the armored shell before latching onto the interior paneling. As the seconds passed, everyone in the area scrambled away with their heads covered, not knowing what to expect, but nothing happened.

Geronimo frowned in disappointment. "Figures," he mumbled.

A few agents boldly approached the car, glancing curiously through the window at the strange projectile. It was shaped like an oversized corkscrew, causing them to chuckle amongst themselves at the alien craftsmanship.

KABOOM!

After an eleven-second delay, the device finally detonated, causing an explosion much larger than anyone could have anticipated. The vehicle atomized as the ground shook, and radiant clouds of hellfire engulfed every agent in range, burning them alive as they writhed in pain, screaming at the top of their lungs. Hovering nearby, the helicopter was almost caught in the blast.

"Holy fuck!" yelled the pilot, pulling away from the flames.

As the entire yard erupted in a frenzy, Geronimo was somewhat stunned. "That's better," he nodded.

"Let's go!" Kali voiced.

Taking advantage of the distraction, she bolted outside toward a steel shack beyond the haze. Following behind, Geronimo ran through the open field, smelling the napalm as he quickly loaded another shell with his eyes on the aircraft. He dropped to one knee, then aimed toward the sky with a steady hand. Glaring down at a world on fire, the pilot had less than a breath to see a masked man ready to shoot. There was a flash of light, then a single shot propelled vertically through the smoke with remarkable speed. The oversized corkscrew ruptured the hull of the aircraft, hitting the pilot like a powerful harpoon through his torso, splattering the cabin with his insides. His eyes rolled back as his head sagged below his shoulders, then the helicopter began careening uncontrollably.

Geronimo stood to his feet, admiring his handiwork, until he noticed the fiery craft was whirling toward him. "Oh shit," he muttered.

He darted in the opposite direction as the copter tumbled wildly through the sky. The tail end struck the control tower, causing it to ricochet before crashing to the earth, exploding on impact in a giant mass of destruction. The force lifted Geronimo off the ground, and as he barreled through the air in a shower of smoldering wreckage, he had a sudden moment of clarity more profound than the prophets. Unfortunately, his epiphany vanished once his head slammed against a rusty crane, rendering him unconscious.

�⚬

Surrounded by scorched alloys and arching flames, Geronimo slowly opened his eyes to a landscape of ashes and embers. His head was swelling with pain, a large metallic shard was lodged deep in his shoulder, and he was covered in soot with smoke rising from the singes on his jacket. Though the duffel bag was still around his neck, the corkscrew cannon was nowhere in sight. Isolated in the middle of hell, he could vaguely hear voices over the sharp ringing in his ears.

"There he is!" someone shouted.

"Get him!" another hollered.

"Fuck," he groaned, crawling across the blackened soil.

Overwhelmed by apocalyptic fire, he slouched against the rusty crane, then clenched his teeth as he painfully yanked the metal shard from his flesh. After tossing the bloody fragment aside, he sorely retracted one of his pistols, then scanned the sweltering battlefield as a lone agent emerged from the haze. Geronimo steadied his gun, but soon realized the man was trying to escape an angry ensemble of vengeful civilians. He watched the agent stumble over his own feet, before they swarmed him like a pack of hungry hyenas, shredding him to pieces in a frenzy of rage and retribution.

Geronimo sat in amazement, simultaneously impressed and disgusted. "Damn," he muttered.

Suddenly, a thunderous sound rattled him from his trance, and a navy-blue truck came soaring through the flames. It quickly maneuvered around several piles of debris as it sped directly toward him, then dramatically drifted to a stop a few yards away. Expecting the worst, he was pleasantly surprised when the passenger door swung open, revealing none other than Kali behind the wheel, grimy and sweaty.

"Come on!" she yelled.

He staggered to his feet, then gratefully fell in the passenger seat without any objection. "Nice truck," he said, admiring the luxurious interior.

"It was Zora's," she replied.

She stomped on the gas pedal, and all four tires kicked up gravel as they fled the scene, barreling through fire and smoke. He gripped tightly onto the grab handle as she swerved between two giant containers, then buckled his seat belt as they accelerated toward the west gate. Passing boxcars and railway equipment, he could hear bursts of gunfire as he stared through the tinted glass. Flocks of people were racing in every direction, fearlessly fighting back like warriors awakened from their slumber, while multiple agents were lost in a sea of hands, consumed by the furious mob. He was witnessing an uprising.

"Hold on!" Kali yelled.

She braced herself as they smashed through a road barrier at the edge of the yard, then made a sharp turn down a narrow avenue behind a series of empty warehouses. The truck slid across the wet pavement as she clenched the wheel, never letting her foot off the gas. Geronimo looked behind them, and two government vehicles were hot on their trail with the sirens blaring.

"We got traffic!" he hollered.

As if on cue, a wave of munitions erupted, forcing Kali to jump the curb as bullets shredded their taillights and rear fender. Flurries of rounds diced the concrete behind them as they raced up the sidewalk, avoiding warped light poles and obsolete newspaper vending machines. She made a hard right at the corner, burning rubber across the street as Geronimo held his guns out the window, desperately returning fire. Speeding down a dark and cluttered road, shots whisked past his ears as he unloaded both magazines, unfortunately to no effect.

"Will you shoot something please!" Kali shouted at him.

He reached inside his duffel bag of tricks for a miracle, and quickly withdrew an assault rifle painted entirely in jungle camouflage. He slapped in a quad-stack magazine full of high velocity rounds, then dangerously propped himself up on the window seal. With his jacket rippling in the rushing air, he aimed the barrel down at the enemy, though it was difficult to keep his balance. As Kali swerved to the opposite end of the street, he held his breath and squeezed the trigger, raining judgment on the closest Suburban. A string of bullets swept across the grille of the car, rupturing the engine and causing it to burst into flames. The vehicle ultimately lost control before veering in front of the other Suburban, resulting in a fiery crash on the roadside.

Geronimo gleefully raised his gun and shouted a war cry, gratified at the sight of their demise. Unfortunately, his celebration was short-lived, considering three armored SUVs surfaced at the next intersection, continuing the pursuit. Swearing under his breath, he did his best to keep them at bay as they bailed through the urban wilds, whipping past iron trees and concrete mountains blocking the sky.

The chase eventually led to the outskirts of downtown, where much of the landscape was under heavy construction. As the winding avenues became more restricted, Kali was forced to navigate the congested tunnels of metal frames and elevated platforms between the many unfinished buildings. Geronimo nearly lost his head as he ducked beneath a steel beam, cursing loudly in the process. He quickly pulled himself back in the passenger seat, then began rummaging through the duffel bag for more options. He finally grabbed two large metallic canisters, then pulled out each of the safety rings as bullets shattered the rear windshield.

"What are you doing?" Kali barked.

"Plan C!" he yelled, popping off the lids.

In an instant, thick streams of red smoke expelled from the cylinders as he held them both out the window, leaving a crimson trail that swiftly engulfed the entire street. Racing through a web of glass and stone, the colorful veil continued to expand, effectively blocking the enemy's line of sight. Their dash lights gleamed like beacons in a sea of smoke that rose above the buildings, causing them to drive blindly into giant rods and tarp-covered fences.

Kali gripped the wheel for an impossible maneuver, and successfully steered the truck into the confined walkway of a narrow work zone. Scraping against the guardrails, she kept her foot on the gas pedal and accelerated up the enclosed path, passing towering pillars and aluminum columns. After charging through a wooden gate, they emerged at the edge of yet another obscured road. Geronimo tossed the canisters to the curb, then looked back to see if they had truly eluded their pursuers.

BANG!

They were suddenly blindsided by a rogue SUV at the corner, launching both vehicles into a dramatic tailspin. Metal and glass crumbled upon impact, and Kali could feel her stomach drop as they hydroplaned uncontrollably across the slick pavement. She slammed on the brakes to no avail, then closed her eyes as they crashed through the entrance of a refurbished shopping center.

Plowing past the automatic doors, the truck barreled over linoleum before smashing into a marble post at the perimeter of a vast lobby. Silence settled amongst the rubble and debris, while clouds of dust curled between thin rays of light piercing from the outside. Much of the truck was damaged beyond repair, yet the engine was still miraculously running. Kali painfully lifted her face off the steering wheel, her forehead seeping with blood. In a disoriented state, she looked over to see Geronimo slumped against the arm rest, his jacket covered in broken glass.

"What the hell just happened," he groaned.

Breathing a sigh of relief, Kali lowered her head in solace, thankful to be alive. Geronimo slowly sat upright, checking for broken bones, then something caught his attention. Staring gravely through the smoke, he saw a wrecked SUV less than twenty feet away. The lights were still flashing, and he could see the driver was gradually gaining consciousness. Kali noticed the same thing, and promptly shifted the truck in reverse. However, as they slowly backed away from the marble obstruction, the agent sluggishly opened his eyes, and immediately opened fire.

A flurry of nine-millimeter rounds showered the hood as Kali ducked below the dashboard, pressing hard on the accelerator. The tires screeched, and they bolted backward through the lobby, fleeing from death's doorstep. Despite his obvious concussion, the well-trained agent initiated the pursuit once again, stepping on the gas with his sidearm out the window. Shots were airborne as both vehicles sped through the vastness of an empty mall, racing past reflective storefront doors embedded in elaborate architecture.

Driving reckless beneath an expansive skylight, Kali was steering rearward with a white-knuckled grip, blinded by the blood in her eye as they bulldozed through a jewelry kiosk. Geronimo desperately raised his rifle to return fire, but the charging handle was stuck, invoking an outburst of extreme profanity. Kali quickly swiped one of his handguns, then began shooting sporadically at the enemy, her reflexes in full control. After avoiding the winding escalators and indoor trees, they propelled through a glass partition, then over a set of marble steps as the exchange of bullets ensued. The agent was relentless, screaming as if possessed with his finger glued to the trigger.

Geronimo was still cursing as he combed the contents of his duffel bag.

"Fuck it!" he gritted. "This what they want, huh? I got something for them!"

At his wit's end, he grabbed an RKG-3EM: a powerful anti-tank grenade. He pulled the pin without hesitation, then leaned out the window, hurling it forward. With their fates in the balance, the grenade cartwheeled through time and space, guided by a single prayer. The drogue parachute was deployed, stabilizing it in mid-flight, before it struck the SUV at a ninety-degree angle, exploding on impact. The crazed agent was instantly engulfed in a sea of fire, and the blast was strong enough to lift the vehicle off the ground, leaving an extravagant trail of cascading flames. The car tumbled through a glass elevator, then slammed against a marble wall, immobilized in a blaze of burning flesh and twisted metal.

"Hell yeah!" Geronimo proudly exclaimed. "Tell the devil I said kiss my ass!"

Although he was grazed in the conflict, his adrenaline made him numb to the pain. He was laughing on the edge of his seat, his eyes on the inferno. However, Kali had yet to slow down, and he eventually looked back to see they were speeding toward a set of automatic doors. Trading his joy for dread, he tensely gripped the dashboard as he held his breath.

"Uh, Kali?" he voiced. "Kali!"

She ignored his cries as they charged backward through the glass like a wrecking ball. The truck stormed over a pedestrian walkway, then swerved across the dark surface of a desolate parking lot before finally screeching to a halt. She shifted gears without saying a word, and the tires burned as they bolted off the curb into the adjacent street, heading for the ruins beyond the freeway.

All was quiet as the seconds crawled into minutes, and Geronimo eventually removed the bandana from his face. He took off his boot, flipped it upside down, and a crinkled blunt fell gently in his lap. He put it to his lips and sparked it aflame, while Kali silently unwrapped her scarf, her mind clearly elsewhere. Crossing another dark intersection, she glanced in the rearview mirror with a tormented heart, thinking of the ones she left behind.

"...She's dead because of me," she whimpered.

Geronimo sat quietly for a moment, then looked at her with sympathetic eyes. "You know that's bullshit," he said, lungs full of smoke.

"You sure about that?" she countered. "How many people have died tonight, huh? How many are dead because of us?"

"Because of *us*?" he choked. "Hold up. We're not the ones killing innocent people. That's what *they* do. They're the problem; they've always been the fucking problem."

"You sure about that? They killed her...they killed her because they thought she was one of us. Don't you get it? All those people...they're dying because of something we started."

Geronimo exhaled a smokestack, mutely watching the buildings scroll past. He had neither the energy nor the desire for a philosophical debate. Nonetheless, her words acted as a catalyst, forcing him to analyze his own perspective.

"You can't walk a straight path in a crooked world," he uttered. "...My mother used to say that. I know it hurts, but there's no high road in this shit. All we can do is survive."

Kali discretely wiped a tear from her cheek. "That ain't enough, Moe," she replied. "Not anymore."

She checked the rearview mirror once again, racing through another ancient section of an abandoned district.

The streets were shimmering like polished floors in the misty night, and Geronimo was blowing smoke in the wind, lost in his own thoughts, looking up at an endless sky with no answer in sight.

CHAPTER THIRTEEN

Fear No Evil

Deep within the ruins of Exposition Park, the Natural History Museum of Los Angeles County had all but been forgotten. In another life, it was one of the largest museums in the west, housing millions of specimens and artifacts that allegedly spanned billions of years. It was a beacon of wonder and discovery. Unfortunately, it was no match for Mother Nature, and much of it was either lost or destroyed in the quake, swallowed by the earth along with its scientific significance. Despite a handful of restoration projects, the damage was far too great, and expenses were above astronomical. Thus, all efforts were eventually abandoned by the city, and the structure remained in limbo.

As time progressed, the man known as Tree Newman became infatuated with the site. Though the SRS never stayed in one place for too long, he wanted to use it as a base of operations. He planned to reinforce the walls with steel, place barricades around entryways, and build a network of secret passages for emergencies. It had enough space for an armory, a training area, barracks for the Soldiers, and a proving ground to test new equipment. However, he was never able to fully implement his vision.

Although the North American Mammal Hall had been converted to a war room, it still housed the remnants of a lost history: the fragmented statue of a large elephant, the scattered bones of a woolly mammoth, the diorama of a rare rhino. However, the chamber had been furnished with posters of bikini models and musicians, an arrangement of chairs and couches, numerous floor-standing speakers, and a black felt pool table to make it livable. Leaning against the wall was an oversized corkboard, littered with candid photographs of crooked cops and dirty politicians.

In the corner of the room, a tattered bison head was resting atop a mahogany table, and Red was staring blankly in its eyes, reclined in the same chair that belonged to his mentor. With one leg propped on the wooden furniture, he was rolling a fat blunt, meditating on Victor's confession. Horse was sitting by the security monitors, cleaning his gun to keep his mind occupied, while Numbers was drinking from a bottle of tequila, questioning everything he had ever known to be true.

"Fuck it, I'm just gonna come out and say it," Numbers announced, breaking the silence. "Look, I know Vic was lying. Right? Right. But what if he wasn't? What if all this...what if it's all really part of some government plot?"

"Do you hear yourself?" Horse countered. "That's what he wanted you to think. That's that government shit; nothing but tricknology."

"True, true," Numbers shrugged. "Don't get it twisted, I know Vic was foul...but all that shit he said about Tree. That's some wild shit. Oh, I meant 'Jeremy Barnes', or whatever the fuck his name was—"

"Don't do that, don't ever fucking do that," Horse demanded, setting the barrel on the table. "Look, before Tree came around, I didn't give a fuck about my life. Hear me? I was in and out of jail. Robbing people, doing drugs, abusing women…shit didn't matter to me. Nothing did, until I heard the man speak. Everything he was saying…it just made sense to me. The Soldiers gave me a purpose, taught me how to live—"

"But what if that's the point?" Numbers interjected. "To give us a purpose, *their* purpose. What if this is how *they* want us to live?"

"Brother, don't let the devil confuse you," Horse replied. "Victor said what he said because he's trained to lie. Besides, you weren't buying that shit when he was selling it. What happened? You feeling different now?"

Numbers took another swig from his bottle of tequila. "Ain't shit different," he gulped. "It's just…some weird shit, I guess. What you think, Red? You ain't said a word since we got back."

"That's because he knows it's bullshit," Horse scoffed.

Red sparked up the leaf, lost in the seclusion of thought. Although he had his doubts, he was haunted by his own paranoia, fully aware that nothing was impossible, and truth could be stranger than fiction. Still, the concept of being controlled without knowing, even manipulated to kill, was something he refused to accept. "Victor was a snake and a traitor," he said coldly. "He deserved worse. As far as I'm concerned, whatever he had to say died with him on that rooftop."

Numbers averted his eyes to the ground, then began to speak with extreme caution. "Red, with all due respect," he shrugged nervously. "I think we should look into this."

"What for?" Horse argued. "It won't change anything. Okay, let's say it's true. Let's say this is all really some government shit. Now what? We're still targets! We're still getting murdered by the pigs!"

"Yeah," Numbers replied. "But wouldn't you want to know the truth?"

Before Horse could respond, their debate was interrupted by a sudden knock at the door. A young woman by the name of Penny sternly entered the room, and she was a prominent member of the SRS Security Council. She had a commanding presence, and was taller than average with a slight muscular build. Her thick braids were laying neatly on her shoulders, and she was wearing a bulletproof vest over a long-sleeved thermal shirt.

"Some of our people are missing," she reported. "Plus, I can't locate the rest of the council. Kali, Rah, Dice, Hayes, and Geronimo are all M.I.A. Nobody's seen them. Something ain't right."

"Perfect," Numbers declared, spilling liquor as he staggered to the corner.

Horse shook his head, showing his concern. "What the hell's going on tonight?" he mumbled.

"More bullshit," Numbers complained. "Add it to the list."

"I need everyone to stay cool," Red stated in a serious tone. "I'm sure they're safe. Any word on Dirt?"

"Dice was supposed to pick him up," she said.

Red massaged his brow with a heavy sigh. "Right, just keep your eyes open. And whenever Dirt shows up, tell him to see me."

Penny could sense the tension in the air as she nodded solemnly. Numbers returned the gesture with his arms crossed, and Horse gave her a two-fingered salute as she exited the room.

Red flicked a few ashes to the floor, then leaned forward with his elbows on the table, digesting the information. "Maybe we *should* look into this," he reluctantly admitted. "But until we do, that rooftop shit stays between us. Understand? I don't want this leaving the room. If there's any truth to it, then we don't know who we can trust."

⋆⟞▬▬◉

Outside the museum, the wind was cold, the air was damp, and the streets were glimmering beneath the moon's ominous glow. Clusters of ash-colored clouds swept across an ebony sky, and a thin mist slowly surfaced from the edge of darkness. As a raven nestled in the crevice of an old building, Dirt was waiting down the block, reclined in a stolen police car, nonchalantly eating a glazed doughnut. He eventually stepped out onto the pavement, then calmly walked toward the museum with a cigarette between his lips. Gathered by the entrance, a dozen Soldiers greeted him with a series of fist bumps, salutes, head nods, and handshakes as he climbed the concrete steps.

"Brother Dirt," someone said.

"I didn't know you was back in town," said another. "Good to see you, brother."

Once inside, he could smell the marijuana in the air, and leaned against a marble pillar as he surveyed the room for familiar faces. All throughout the expansive foyer, people were

141

lounging on plush furniture sets, eating and talking amongst themselves, sharing fat blunts and pouring out liquor as soulful tunes resonated from an impressive sound system. The great room appeared to be boundless in space, with multiple graffiti murals stretching endlessly across the towering walls. Brass chandeliers radiated a warm light from the high rafters, and oriental rugs were arranged symmetrically on the vast travertine floors. At the center was a portrait of Tree Newman, accented with bundles of flowers, glowing incense sticks, and aromatic candles.

A young man by the name of Spades was sitting at a nearby table, taking shots of whiskey in solitude. Although he had the face of a child, he had the wisdom of an elder: he was the Minister of Information. His military helmet matched his varsity jacket, and his revolver was in a leather holster at the hip, like a gunslinger from the old west. He could see Dirt approaching from the corner of his eye, and a rare smile appeared on his face. "Aw shit, the champ's here," he declared.

Dirt met him with a dap, then sat beside him with a humble grin. "Peace, brother," he voiced. "How've you been?"

"Shit, can't complain," Spades groaned.

"Another day in paradise, huh?" said Dirt.

Spades refilled his glass, then finished it in one gulp. "Shit never changes," he grimaced. "I'm surprised to see you, though. I thought you'd be long gone by now."

"Not yet. Still got some business to take care of."

Spades poured a separate cup for his colleague, then replenished his own for another round. "You know Red's gonna be pissed when you leave," he said, spilling a few drops on the table.

Dirt gladly consumed the liquor in a few swigs. "He'll get over it," he winced, embracing the fire in his belly.

"Guess he'll have to," Spades chuckled.

As they continued to drink, Spades became fixated on Tree's portrait. "You see this shit?" he pointed. "See how they do us? They'll take your family, your land, your history, your culture, your language, your religion, your livelihood, then turn around and call *you* a terrorist. Ain't that some shit? But that's how the devil operates. Tree knew what it was. He knew the truth. And they killed him for it…"

Dirt lit another cigarette, then leaned back in a thick cloud of nicotine. "That's some real shit," he exhaled.

"It's fucked up. And if they don't kill you, they'll assassinate your character. They'll call you crazy, or a radical, or a racist, or a thug, or whatever. They'll say whatever they say, and people will believe it. That's how it always goes…"

Dirt could hear the tribulation in his tone, and was empathetic as he replied with compassion. "You're forgetting one thing, brother," he said, reaching for the bottle of whiskey. "They can't kill your spirit."

He poured another round for them both, and Spades managed to smile despite himself. "To Tree," he announced, raising his glass. "The man that knew the truth."

Dirt mirrored the gesture with a smirk, and after sharing a drink in Tree's honor, he was in a definitive state of inebriation. Soaking in the ambiance, all sensations faded to the background.

Suddenly, a strong hand seized him by the shoulder with an iron grip. It was Penny, standing over him with a disgruntled expression on her face. "So, this is where you've been hiding," she hissed, tightening her grasp. "At the bottom of a bottle. Why am I not surprised?"

He wrestled away from her cobra clutch, while Spades calmly poured himself another drink. "Good to see you, Penny," he slurred.

"I know it is," she acknowledged, still glaring at Dirt. "Red's looking for you. You're supposed to check in the moment you get back. And where the hell's Dice?"

"No clue; he wasn't at the station," Dirt frowned, rubbing his shoulder. "Which is very rude, by the way. I had to walk. Remind me to hit him with a chair when I see him."

Spades almost choked trying not to laugh, but Penny was clearly not amused. There was a subtle shift in her attitude, as if a fire had been doused in her spirit.

Although Dirt was highly intoxicated, it was obvious something was troubling her. "I'm just playing," he said. "I'll probably just throw him through a window."

"You don't get it, do you?" she voiced. "You're over here cracking jokes, but no one's fucking laughing." She dismally shook her head, then stormed off without saying another word.

"Damn, maybe we should be worried," Spades noted.

Dirt drunkenly rose to his feet with an air of trepidation. "You're in America," he said, passing him two cigarettes. "Being worried comes with the territory."

Spades accepted his offering with a wry smirk. "Take care of yourself, champ."

"Stay safe, brother."

The two exchanged dap as a sign of respect, then Dirt reeled toward the opposite end of the hall, conversing with his fellow patrons along the way. As he navigated through the clouds of ganja and pools of liquor, he eagerly stopped for anyone willing to share. By the time he reached the stairwell, he was proudly seeing double. With a plastic cup veering in his hand, he laughed helplessly as he staggered on, delighted by his own insobriety. After stumbling outside the war room, he could hear voices from behind the door, though they were muffled and indistinct. Everything around him was spinning, and following a futile attempt to clear his head, he eventually knocked twice before finally crossing the threshold.

"Hola," he announced upon intrusion.

Numbers turned around with a startled expression. "This motherfucker right here," he mumbled, clutching his bottle of tequila.

They embraced with a handshake and one-armed hug, then Dirt casually took a seat next to Horse at the table, who was intently rolling blunts by a purple mountain of marijuana. He respectfully acknowledged Dirt with a slight nod, though his eyes never swayed from the task at hand. Dirt returned the gesture, while Red simply shook his head with an irritated expression.

"Are we having a good time?" he frowned.

Dirt glanced across the table with a faint smile. "I got here as soon as I could," he explained. "Traffic's a bitch."

Red reclined with his hands folded in his lap. "You and Dice had some trouble?"

"Yeah, he never showed up," Dirt shrugged. "But you know how he is. He's probably laid up with some female as we speak."

An awkward silence spread throughout the room, and while Horse sparked the clotted leaf aflame, Numbers was slumped in a nearby chair with his face in his palms.

Red nodded warily, disturbed by the news. "Maybe," he said ominously. "These are treacherous times. Every move has to be right and exact; we can't afford to make mistakes. It's imperative that we stay on point, now more than ever."

"Absolutely," Dirt assented.

"Anyway, I'm glad you're safe," Red told him.

"Likewise."

"No doubt. So, with that being said, tell me you got some good news."

Dirt waited for Horse to pass him the burning blunt, then inhaled deeply before he spoke. "Not exactly," he choked. "I think we've been excommunicated…"

Red furrowed his brow, unable to hide his frustration. "What the fuck are you talking about?" he scowled.

"Well, I went out there like you said," Dirt described. "But now that Tree's gone, no one wants to fuck with us. The Black Stars, the Midnight Marauders…they wouldn't even have a sit-down."

"Are you fucking kidding me?" Red shouted, jumping to his feet. "I don't believe this shit! We've helped them out more times than I can count!"

"So much for reinforcements," Numbers murmured.

"Benedict Arnold motherfuckers," Horse grumbled, lighting another blunt.

"After all the blood we've shed?" Red continued, pacing across the room. "Where's the fucking loyalty in that, huh? Fucking cowards!"

"No doubt, but there's more," Dirt asserted. "There's a small group up north. They're underground, so they're hard to find. But they're young, angry, and ready to fight. They're willing to have a powwow, but they want to meet with you personally."

Red narrowed his eyes as he stood quietly by the table. "They seem legit to you?" he asked.

Dirt drew a worn piece of paper from his back pocket. "It's not like we have too many options," he said, placing the frayed note on the table. "But whatever you decide to do, this is how to reach them."

Somewhat discouraged, Red pocketed the document as he returned to his seat. "Everything's always a fucking gamble," he uttered.

Moments after he spoke, Penny abruptly marched through the door. "Look who's here!" she announced gleefully.

Following her disruptive declaration, Geronimo and Kali valiantly entered the room, emerging like two warriors returning from the edge of hell. Covered in blood and soot, they were survivors of a concrete inferno, a dangerous land full of loose cannons and lost souls. They had been forged in the flames of violence, hardened by the elements of war, and the nightmare reflected prominently in their eyes. Everyone was so awestruck by their weathered appearance, that when Geronimo intercepted the blunt in rotation, his actions went uncontested. He sat atop the table with the poise of a grandmaster, his demeanor stone cold as he slowly inhaled the potion.

"What the fuck?" Red glared. "...You look like shit."

"We're lucky to be alive," Kali interjected. "Long story short, we're all in danger. We need to leave right fucking now."

She could feel their eyes upon her, as if being examined under a microscope.

"Well, that's one way to get my attention," Red scrutinized.

Kali boldly proceeded with her report, her composure solid and steadfast. She told them the horrid tale of Bunchy, about his shop getting raided by a death squad of federal agents, and the unfortunate demise of his cousin. She told them of the nightmare that was Maywood, about the refugee camp getting destroyed, and an old friend dying in her arms. She spoke about their narrow escape from death, standing as living proof of her testimony, and the earth-shattering news had everyone suspended in their own despair.

"…Motherfucker," Red voiced, lost in dismay.

"My thoughts exactly," Geronimo exhaled. "This whole shit's been compromised. Who knows how many spots got raided; but we should assume the worst."

Penny was standing tentatively by the door. "That would explain why we have people missing," she mumbled.

As Dirt rose pensively from his chair, Horse and Numbers exchanged worrisome glances.

"Red, we can't stay here," Kali asserted. "They could be heading this way…"

After listening to her words, Red quietly stroked the hairs on his chin, reflecting on the powers that be. These were the tactics of a relentless beast, an institution of extreme evil, and the more he thought about it, the more furious he became. Whether it was virtuous or vanity, he refused to submit. He would never surrender, nor retreat, and his conviction was prominent in his eyes. "I'm sorry about your friend," he said eventually. "I really am. She deserved better…they all did. But if those pigs ever get bold enough to come around here, I'm returning all those motherfuckers in a bag. Trust. That's what ammo's for."

"Have you even been listening?" said Geronimo in disbelief. "Red, these ain't your average alphabet boys. We're talking next-level military shit. They stormed that camp like a goddamn beach in Normandy. You feel me?"

"Yeah, sounds like they're getting desperate," Red affirmed.

"Sounds more like you got a death wish," Geronimo countered.

"On the contrary," Red replied. "If death comes for me, he better be strapped."

"Nice quote," Geronimo scoffed. "Maybe they'll put that on your tombstone."

"Are you two finished?" Kali interrupted. "Because all this macho shit's getting old."

As Geronimo cursed in defiance, Red stood to his feet, his disposition chiseled in stone.

"Remember, soldier boy, we both got one foot in the grave. But I don't run from devils. Devils run from me."

"Great, we get it," Kali hissed. "You want to stick around? Fine, fuck it. You're bulletproof. But at least tell me you got a plan if they show up."

"Yeah, kill them," Red stated coldly. "Now, if you'll excuse me, certain matters require my attention."

He sternly made his exodus with a revitalized sense of determination. Penny, Numbers, and Horse apprehensively followed suit, whereas Dirt stayed behind, alongside Kali and Geronimo. As they lingered in silence, Kali slouched against the wall with her chin down, gravely contemplating their fate.

CHAPTER FOURTEEN

Before the Dawn

It was an hour before sunrise, and the atmosphere in the museum was strangely serene. Shadows were dancing in the silence, and many of the Soldiers had fallen asleep, too intoxicated to function. However, Geronimo was wide awake, sitting in a small gallery above the foyer. Next to a bottle of water and a freezer bag full of colorful herbs, he was slouched in a theater seat, smoking and meditating on the future. With his knife twirling in one hand, he found himself haunted by the unknowable, taunted by the intangible.

"You can lose an eye like that," said Dirt, sitting beside him with a six-pack.

Geronimo caught the blade with his fingertips. "It helps me think," he replied.

"Of course it does," Dirt chuckled. "Where's Kali?"

Geronimo stared intently over the banister. "I think she needs some time," he alluded, clearing his lungs. "…She's been through a lot."

Dirt popped open a can of beer, then leaned back with a heavy sigh. "Look, I didn't get to speak on it earlier," he voiced, slurping from the canister. "...I guess I was still processing everything. But I'm glad you're okay. I can't imagine what it was like for you out there."

Geronimo tilted his head back, encompassed in smoke. "Yeah, life can be a real fucking treat sometimes," he exhaled.

"Seriously," Dirt persisted. "I don't know what I'd do...if something ever happened to you."

Geronimo caught himself after hearing the tone in his brother's voice. "Hey, I'm good," he asserted. "Nothing but a few bumps and bruises. Maybe some new bullet wounds. But that's like breakfast for me. They're like vitamins now, it's how I get my iron."

Shaking his head, Dirt laughed quietly to himself. "Bullets for breakfast," he grinned. "But you won't eat pork."

Geronimo pointed his knife in an authoritative manner. "You know I don't fuck with the swine," he stated.

"I blame Grandad for that. Mama always cooked bacon..."

"Yeah, but it was turkey."

"Nah, it was pork."

Geronimo looked at him sideways. "That's bullshit," he said.

"I'm telling you; it was pork."

"Whatever," Geronimo scowled. "You were too young to remember anyway."

"You're only older than me by a few minutes," Dirt shrugged.

"Seven," Geronimo noted. "Seven minutes."

The fraternal twins shared a short laugh, and Geronimo was starting to relax as he rolled another leaf, enjoying the good company and conversation. He listened as Dirt romanticized the tale of defending Tree's mural, then glamorize the rescue of two teenagers, describing every detail with more emphasis than a sports announcer. His brother always had the best stories, ever since they were children.

"That's easily the coolest shit I've heard all week," Geronimo told him, beaming with pride. "Those fucking cops had it coming."

"Yeah," Dirt belched, crumbling an empty can. "I'd be lying if I said I didn't enjoy it."

Geronimo finished sealing the blunt, then placed it between his lips. "I probably would've just shot the motherfuckers," he confessed, flicking his lighter.

Dirt laughed to himself, then everything slowly started to spin. After drinking all night, his senses finally liquified into a composition of muddled sounds and images. He closed his eyes and slumped down in his seat, spanning the cosmos of his own subconscious.

"Listen...you know I'm leaving," he mumbled, his chin on his chest. "And I really think you should reconsider. It'll be like the old days. Just you and me, bro. Fuck this war. Life shouldn't be like this..."

Geronimo reclined in a pool of smoke, torn between his logic and emotion. "Shit used to be different," he uttered. "The food programs, the self-defense classes, the clinics. It really felt like we were doing something good...something positive."

"And look at us now," Dirt added bitterly.

"No shit," Geronimo agreed, inhaling the potion. "...But I don't know, man."

Dirt slightly raised his head, his eyes virtually closed. "It's cool, I get it," he chuckled.

Geronimo glanced at him sideways. "Get *what?*" he questioned.

"Come on, bro," Dirt sighed. "Stop playing. You care about her. Just admit it."

Geronimo glared at his twin, then looked away before helplessly grinning like a schoolboy. "Shit, maybe," he said. "She's different. She's one of the strongest people I know, but she's delicate at the same time. She has a good heart, but she's not afraid to get her hands dirty. She's smart, she's fearless... she looks good without makeup..."

"Sounds like a keeper," Dirt smiled.

"No doubt," Geronimo nodded, passing the burning leaf. "But she's dedicated, you know? She's devoted to this shit. She really cares about her people."

Dirt meticulously plucked the blunt with his fingertips. "Sounds like Mama," he slurred, taking a hit.

Geronimo stared at him with a twisted expression. "Don't be weird," he frowned. "That's fucking weird."

Dirt almost choked as he buckled over in laughter. "I'm just saying!" he coughed. "That last part sounded like Mama. How's that weird?"

"Stop it, don't ever repeat that shit," Geronimo replied, shaking his head.

As he emptied the tobacco out another cigar, Dirt sunk in his seat with his mind on the future. "Love's a good thing to have, try not to lose it," he mumbled.

"Love's a strong word."

"That's because it's important," Dirt belched. "...Especially these days." He slowly staggered to his feet, then waited for his equilibrium to regain balance.

"Where're you going?" Geronimo shrugged.

"I already told you. I'm leaving."

He reached out to his brother, and Geronimo rose from his chair, somewhat bewildered. "Damn, I didn't know you meant right now," he confessed.

"No time like the present."

Giving his twin a dap and a hug, Dirt held onto his brother for a few extra seconds, then reluctantly let him go. He turned away and began reeling down the aisle, stumbling over his own feet, ashes cascading to the floor.

"Hey…I'll catch up with you," Geronimo promised him. "Just…try to stay out of trouble."

"That definitely sounds like Mama," Dirt said playfully. As he swayed across the dusty carpet, he pointed back at his brother with a heartfelt grin. "To be continued," he told him.

"To be continued," Geronimo affirmed.

Dirt passed under the archway of the balcony, then disappeared behind a veil of shadows, leaving Geronimo alone in a silhouette of smoke.

As clusters of dark clouds enveloped a vanishing moon, the Black Hawks were waiting anxiously near the leveled Memorial Coliseum, ready for the inevitable, hungry for the inescapable. Inside the transport, Rico was staring at a digital screen, using fiber optic cameras to survey the museum. Primed for battle, he was watching the Soldiers, tracking their every move, observing like a predator from the shadows.

"Hey, Tin Man," Dozer huffed. "You admiring the scenery, or what? Let's get this show on the road. The sooner we do this; the sooner I get my money."

Maverick was drinking coffee from a thermos, fantasizing about their future fortune. "Ah, the true motivator," he voiced. "I think I might buy a boat."

Sparks was in a meditative state, visualizing their victory. "You already have a boat," she smirked.

"You can never have too many boats," Maverick grinned.

"Shit, after this you can buy a whole fleet," said Junior. "As for me, I'm buying a house on the beach…in Fiji."

"Nice," Hennessy chimed.

Annoyed by the banter, Rico continued his surveillance with a scowl. His true incentive was the accumulation of power, not wealth. If the mission was a success, he was guaranteed unlimited upgrades to his augmentations, giving him the strength and speed of a hundred men. He would be a god, a mighty force on the earth, dominating all who oppose his will. Ever since his completion of the "Titan" program, this was his only desire, though he would never disclose it to a single soul.

Electricity was in the air, and time became elusive as the mercenaries prepared to engage, double-checking their gear.

"It's time," Rico announced.

"Finally!" Dozer rejoiced, cracking his knuckles.

"Most of them are in the main hall," Rico explained, strapping on his helmet. "So, once we're in, we hit them hard. No prisoners."

Sparks injected herself with a powerful enhancement shot, amplifying her senses. "How many?" she gritted.

"A few dozen."

"That's it?" Hennessey scoffed, loading his firearm. "We'll be done before breakfast."

"Don't underestimate them," Rico insisted. "...But once it's over, pancakes are on me."

"That's what I'm talking about!" Junior rejoiced.

"But I wanted waffles," Maverick complained.

"Just keep your guns up and stay sharp," Rico ordered. "Now, hold onto your asses."

With the push of a button, the eight-wheeled death machine began accelerating through the ruins of Exposition Park, reaching an excessive speed before launching a lethal cluster bomb. It released six miniature rockets, all guided by an advanced tracking system, and the glowing projectiles braided hot strings of smoke as they streamlined between the trees, spiraling over broken terrain. In rapid succession, the chain of missiles collided with the museum, rupturing the decrepit walls, and causing a drastic series of explosions. Numerous Soldiers were instantly killed in the bombardment, consumed by clouds of heat and debris.

At the opposite end, the violent sequence jarred Geronimo from his slumber as bursts of fire flooded inside the foyer. Frozen in place, his worst nightmare unfolded as a monster-sized tank came crashing through the flames. As people were scrambling and screaming, the metal monstrosity rumbled to a fiery halt at the center of the main hall, glitching between states of visibility. A heavy machine gun extended from its shell, then began firing eight-thousand rounds per minute in a swift rotary motion, sweeping throughout the chamber.

Flurries of bullets diced through the air, and multitudes of Soldiers were swallowed by a relentless wave of ammunition. Unable to escape, they shattered into wet compounds and particles, like flesh balloons filled with fluids. The museum had become a slaughterhouse, and Tree's image was ripped to slivers as bodies stacked upon bodies, producing mounds of dead men and women brave enough to take a stand. Crawling behind the banister, Geronimo was helpless in the onslaught, his eyes swelling with tears. After an eternity of hell, the machine gun finally ceased fire, and all that remained were the silent sounds of the grave.

In a sweltering circle of smoke, the Black Hawks exited the transport, then walked casually among the killing fields. They were surrounded by faces of death, floating in gardens of gray matter, overflowing with dismembered remnants of unidentifiable body parts.

Grimly shaking his head, Dozer looked down at the scarlet leftovers of a severed woman. "What a waste," he muttered. "That was too easy."

"You sound disappointed," said Rico, nudging a cadaver with his boot.

"I was expecting more," Dozer replied. "All that hype for nothing."

"It's called the 'path of least resistance'," Sparks grinned. "It's the only way to travel."

Laying in the shadows, Geronimo could hear their chatter from the balcony. They were laughing and making jokes, satirizing and mocking the dead. It was enough to make his stomach turn as he angrily wiped the sorrow from his face, seized by an excess of violent rage.

As the mercenaries bragged amongst themselves, they neglected to see a lone Soldier, emerging from a red sea of bodies. It was Spades, lurking in the aftermath with his six-shooter in hand. Mortally wounded, his garments were wet with blood as he waded through the remains of his brethren, fighting for every breath. Death was imminent as he pointed his gun at the invaders, and valiantly squeezed the trigger. A slug struck Rico in the back, who immediately turned around with his rifle at the shoulder, targeting the assailant. The mercenaries promptly opened fire with their advanced weaponry, and the merciless barrage acted as a meat grinder, drowning Spades in a hot soup of his former self.

Geronimo cringed at the sight, lowering his head with an unspoken prayer. He left his duffel bag in the war room, and with neither a plan nor a strategy, this was unlike anything he had ever encountered. He was astronomically outgunned, the museum was ablaze, and Kali was still somewhere on the premises. He imagined her in the hands of these murderers, and he feared for her life more than his own. He began shadowing the invaders from above, creeping along the aisles without making a sound, thankful his brother left when he did.

"Hey, Tin Man," Dozer heckled. "Maybe you should get some eyes on the back of your head."

The team of assassins approached the stairwell, then divided into two groups. The first squad consisted of Rico, Dozer, and Junior; the second unit comprised of Sparks, Maverick, and Hennessy. Sparks led her faction toward the east end, while Rico and his company ascended to the second level. After reaching the top landing, the trio advanced in a triangular formation, blending with the slanted shadows, passing fantastical portraits and replicated beasts. Nefarious and diabolical, they moved like a plague in the darkness, destined to destroy.

However, Geronimo was no stranger to stealth. Circumventing their line of sight, he disappeared behind an elaborate foliage display, utilizing a secret passage. The narrow pathway was dark, humid, and reeked of mildew, yet it allowed him to stalk his enemy with ease. As they navigated from room to room, he watched them through the cracks and crevices in the walls. Studying them like a scientist, he hoped to discover their weakness, including a method to exploit it. Considering their body armor made them invulnerable to bullets, he figured a much more radical approach would be necessary.

⤳═●

On the first level, Sparks and her team were traversing a labyrinth of dark hallways, seeking out souls for the fire. Thermal scopes guided them through the unknowable, raising hairs at every twist and turn as they searched for any remaining opposition. After reaching the end of another long corridor, Maverick checked inside a nearby restroom, while Hennessy maintained his position. Sparks approached a large pair of impact doors, then pushed one ajar with the tip of her rifle. Covertly, a thin black wire was connected to the latch on the other side, and she spotted it as it snapped.

"Get back!" she hollered, running in the opposite direction.

BOOM!

The severed wire detonated an explosive attached to the interior bottom rail, resulting in a blast that lifted her clear off the ground. She flipped head-over-heels in a geyser of rubble, then landed on her back as smoke emanated off her body armor. Hennessy rushed to her aid, then a sudden gust of gunfire erupted from beyond the smoldering hole in the wall, forcing them to scramble behind the casing of an adjacent doorway.

"You fuckers!" Horse hollered, squeezing the trigger of a massive M60.

With his weapon mounted on a tripod, the ammunition belt quickly disintegrated as he unloaded a merciless sum of projectiles, yelling at the top of his lungs over each deafening discharge. A violent hurricane blanketed the area, rupturing through marble and stone until the very last cartridge. Afterward, he picked up the smoking gun, then bolted out of sight. Maverick was still hugging the floor, drowning in dust and debris. He peeped around the corner of the bathroom entrance, then carefully regrouped with his other teammates.

"What the hell was that?" Rico voiced over the radio. "Sounded like a bomb."

"Looks like we got a few stragglers," Sparks grumbled over the radio.

"How exciting," Rico transmitted. "Take care of it."

Meanwhile, Horse was sweating bullets alongside a handful of the last remaining Soldiers. Hiding in a damp storage room, they were armed with shotguns and assault rifles, ready for the next life. They were encompassed by artifacts packed in giant crates; their cultural significance already forgotten. Numbers was crouched by a prosthetic Olmec head, holding a German firearm with a look of desperation. He glanced at Horse, who nodded at him with a subtle air of respect, and the two shared an unspoken understanding as they rallied for the showdown.

A moment passed before a pair of smoke grenades spiraled into the room, skipping across the floor. Cumulus clouds expanded, and a firmament of white smoke quickly spread throughout the chamber, carrying with it a deadly neurotoxin. The effect was instantaneous, causing blindness and suffocation as their insides began to boil. Drowning in darkness, Horse collapsed to one knee, choking on his own liquids, while Numbers was paralyzed in a vacuum of pain, bleeding from every orifice. They were helpless in the chemical attack, ending in a gruesome and agonizing death for them all. The deadly nerve gas slowly evaporated, then the mercenaries casually entered the room wearing protective masks.

Sparks nudged a bloated body with the nose of her weapon. "It's been taken care of," she reported apathetically.

"Perfect," Rico transmitted. "Now, keep searching and stay on your toes. No more surprises, understand?"

"Copy that," Sparks acknowledged. "We're heading for the east wing."

After exiting the horrendous gas chamber, they backtracked across the smoldering lobby, passing gold and red flames licking at the dead. They continued toward the once vibrant "Becoming Los Angeles" exhibit, where much of the area had been scavenged for materials, exposing the beams and joists in the walls and floor. The air was hot, and the plywood creaked beneath their boots as they explored the ghostly grounds. There were still remnants of historic figurines and miniature models next to various power tools and construction equipment, frozen ominously in the shadows. Surprisingly, the pulse of a classic breakbeat began swelling in the distance, alerting the deadly trio.

"What the fuck is that?" hissed Hennessy.

"I think that's Public Enemy," Maverick whispered.

"Will you two shut the hell up?" Sparks grumbled.

Staying low, she guided her squad toward the infectious rhythm. They were walking on eggshells, sticking to the walls in anticipation of another attack. Chasing phantoms in the dark, the music was getting louder and louder, causing Hennessy to feel nauseous. Suddenly disoriented, he stopped momentarily to gather his bearings, unaware that the deafening music was cloaking a sub-sonic frequency, specifically designed to attack the equilibrium. His eardrums were throbbing as he buckled over in a cold sweat, staggered and stupefied. "...What's happening?" he gritted.

Secretly, Kali was laying in the crawl space beneath the floorboards, holding a drill gun and a controller for the micro speakers she placed around the room. Wearing noise-canceling headphones, she was installing cartridge traps with seven-hundred grain bullets directly below his feet. She rigged one more high-powered round between the wooden panels, then shimmied away on her back without being detected. In a daze, Hennessy carelessly stumbled upon the trap, and his weight pressed the bullet down against the firing pin, igniting the primer.

In an instant, the thunderous round propelled upward through the rubber sole of his boot, causing the bottom portion of his leg to explode. Chunks of meat and streams of blood flooded the floor as he toppled over, dismembered and screaming violently. He squirmed across the plywood with nowhere to go, only to place his hand atop another cartridge trap. Consequently, everything below his elbow ruptured open, and he lost consciousness as he gradually bled to death. In conjunction, his comrades were also afflicted by the enigmatic sonic weapon, and Maverick had collapsed near an altar dedicated to the city, regurgitating in his safety mask, while Sparks was on her knees in a state of paralysis.

Seizing the opportunity, Kali arose from an access panel in the floor, then marched toward her enemies with the drill gun still in hand. Standing over an incapacitated Maverick, she pulled his head back and shoved the power tool under his chin, gruesomely grinding through flesh and bone until she struck brain matter. Thirsting for vengeance, she was drenched in his blood by the time she yanked the tool from his cranium. Afterward, she headed for Sparks with the same murderous intentions, who was helpless as death personified came for her from the deep. Her helmet was ripped off, and the last thing she ever saw was the drill inches from her retina.

⊷═◉

On the second level, Geronimo was still in dangerous territory. He tracked his enemy through the remains of the Hall of Birds, where the walls were covered with faded paintings of jungles and tropical landscapes. Artificial vegetation sprouted from the rubble of a crumbling roof, and extinct winged creatures were perched atop plastic trees draped over empty basins.

"This place's starting to creep me out," Junior mentioned, awed by their surroundings.

"Sparks, can you hear me?" Rico relayed. "Sparks!"

"Something ain't right," Dozer snarled. "We should probably get down there."

Him and Rico immediately headed for the east wing, while Junior was somewhat sluggish to react, giving Geronimo the perfect chance to strike. Moving with the speed and stealth of a panther, he swiftly pounced upon Junior, grappling him with a sleeper hold while covering his mouth. He then used his blade to brutally impale the jugular, and they both fell to the floor. Junior was kicking and flailing as they wrestled on the ground, but Geronimo firmly held the knife in place, until his prey eventually went limp.

After shoving the corpse aside with a grunt, Geronimo cleaned his knife with the dead man's uniform, then helped himself to some newfound equipment. Along with the mercenary's rifle, he marveled at a plethora of next generation grenades, each with adhesive capabilities. He selected them all before disappearing into the shadows once again, this time with more confidence.

Rico was already at the stairs before he realized someone was missing. "Hold it," he said. "Where the hell's Junior?"

"I thought he was behind us," Dozer griped.

Fire was spreading throughout the museum, and Rico could see the flames closing in. "I don't like this," he voiced. "Feels like this shit's starting to go sideways."

"No shit, I told you that kid's off his meds."

"Listen," Rico ordered. "I'll check on the other team. When you find Junior, regroup with us at the transport. We're getting the hell out of here; I think we've done enough damage."

He ventured down into the smoky foyer, while Dozer reluctantly retraced their steps, crossing the same murky corridors. Carrying his weapon at the shoulder, he finally reached the exhibit where Junior was last seen, and silently searched for his colleague, careful to not make a sound. Suddenly, he had the feeling he was being watched, and glanced over his shoulder to see a dark figure rushing him from the shadows. With his finger on the trigger, he quickly turned around and opened fire, shooting at the darkness. "You're a bold one; I'll give you that!" he yelled. "But that don't impress me!"

Dodging death by an inch, Geronimo bailed behind a taxidermized eagle as a tsunami of bullets diced through the air. Bursts of ammunition exploded through the fake trees and hills, scattering clusters of colorful fragments in the atmosphere.

"In fact, I'm kind of disappointed!" Dozer continued, aiming at the elusive phantom. "They said you were killers!"

Continuously avoiding his own demise, Geronimo rapidly returned fire as he scrambled from one foliage display to another, forcing Dozer to seek cover of his own. It was a ballet of bullets as the two traded rounds, unloading without mercy, transforming the hall into rubble. Pockets of wreckage soared amongst the destruction, and each man was struggling to stay ahead of the line of fire. Racing from cover to cover, Geronimo rolled behind one of the last standing barriers, out of ammunition and surrounded by smoldering debris. There was a moment of silence, then Dozer stepped out from behind a tattered support column.

"Dead yet?" he laughed, walking over shell casings. "I can't believe I'm getting paid for this shit. I haven't even broken a sweat."

As he loaded another magazine, Geronimo had less than a second to act, and swiftly charged at his enemy like a force of nature. Aiming for the neck, he hurled his knife through the darkness, but Dozer managed to duck the poisonous reach of the blade. However, he failed to recover fast enough for Geronimo's leaping push-kick, and the sole of a boot landed against his chest harder than a sledgehammer. His shoulders practically touched as he stumbled backward across the room, fumbling his weapon in the process. With a sharp pain resonating deep in his sternum, he desperately reached for his sidearm, but Geronimo quickly unleashed a series of lethal combinations, relentlessly striking joints and pressure points with extreme intensity.

Dozer was trapped in a perfect storm of immaculate power and technique, a demonstration of brutality and speed. Ultimately, his trachea was crushed by a furious flying knee, severing all airflow to his lungs, and he folded over like a wet piece of paper. Geronimo stepped aside after chopping down the giant, then casually helped himself to more ammunition.

"Looks like you broke more than a sweat," he muttered.

⊷⇒

Rico was racing through chambers of ghosts, calling out in the smoke as the temperature steadily increased.

"Dozer!" he yelled frantically. "Dozer, report! Sparks! Anyone! Someone talk to me!" He turned another fiery corner, then a voice cloaked in static pierced his eardrum.

"Rico," said the voice. "Rico, can you hear me?"

Rico stopped dead in his tracks, his eyes wide with concern.

"Oh...uh...Mr. Heidrich, sir," he stammered.

Dr. Eugene Heidrich was the CEO and owner of Heidrich Core Industries, or "Hydricore" for short. Labeled an eccentric by his competitors, he was in fact a brilliant man, a mathematician who specialized in computer science and biotechnology. Building his company from the ground up, he imagined a technological utopia, a future without bounds, and had accumulated enough power and wealth to implement his vision. He had been watching through a camera implanted in Rico's retina, as well as various micro cameras placed within the Black Hawks' body armor.

"Rico, I need you to listen to me very carefully," Heidrich continued. "Your entire team has been eliminated; please return to the transport for immediate extraction."

"What?" Rico blurted in disbelief.

"It's unfortunate, I know," said Heidrich apathetically. "But these things happen."

Rico could hardly process what he was hearing. "How is this possible?"

"They were weak, but that's irrelevant. You did good, Rico. Consider this a victory."

Rico was beyond reach, lost and dumbfounded, alone in a world that was upside down. "Sir, with all due respect, how the fuck is this a victory?" he snapped.

"I'm afraid you're missing the big picture," Heidrich replied. "But that's okay. You're paid to kill, not to think. Now, return to the transport. Your payment has already been wired to your account."

As Rico stood in the haze, struggling to understand, his true desire remained chiseled in stone. "Sir, what about my upgrades?" he said.

"Well, obviously the Soldiers have not been entirely neutralized. Which was a stipend based on our personal agreement, if you recall."

"Then it's not over yet," Rico grumbled.

"Maybe you didn't hear me. So, allow me to assist you. You are not in charge. Your only job is to follow orders; *my* orders. So, get your ass back to the transport, or I'll have it stripped for parts. Understand?"

Rico shook his head with a scowl on his face. "…Copy that," he lied.

⋅◦≡◉

At the far end of the east wing, Red was sitting on the floor of the grand rotunda, resting beneath a cracked statue of a praying angel. It was almost dawn, and he was bleeding from a massive bullet wound above his hip, isolated in an intimate darkness. His eyes were empty, as if the life was drained from his spirit. With a cigarette between his lips and a gun by his side, he was sweating from the pain as he inhaled more nicotine.

He had been in the foyer when all hell broke loose, and only managed to survive by hiding amongst the dead. After pulling himself away from the mountain of his mutilated brothers and sisters, he wandered the corridors in a state of dismay, bleeding out until Penny found him near an old dinosaur exhibit, lying on a pile of bones. He had been blinded by pride, disillusioned by grand visions of honor and glory, and deceived by majestic tales of noble sacrifice. Because of his vanity, lives were lost, blood was spilled, and an entire movement had been desolated.

He suddenly heard footsteps, and quickly pointed his gun at the unknown, but was relieved to see Kali emerge from the shadows.

"What the hell?" she whispered, raising her hands in peace. "Are you crazy? Why didn't you leave with the others?"

Red lowered his sidearm with a bloody grin. "I had to make sure you got out okay," he exhaled. "I guess the sound bomb worked…"

"Stupid," Kali grunted, helping him off the ground. "I'm getting you out of here."

Earlier, she had been outside shooting liquor bottles in solitude, and was fortunate enough to have missed the initial attack. Nonetheless, upon the invasion, she bravely sought survivors amongst the rubble, but there were too many bodies, and only a handful were saved from the flames. She boldly led them through the fire, and once they reached the rotunda, the small group of Soldiers fled the museum, escaping through the ruins of the USC campus. However, she refused to leave without Geronimo, while Red felt an obligation to them both.

"Listen," he grimaced, leaning on Kali for support. "Whatever happens...you were right. You were right about everything. But there's something you should know—"

"Save it," she gritted, carrying him toward the exit. "It doesn't matter anymore."

⊶⊸⊙

As fire consumed the museum, Geronimo was creeping through the shambles of the west wing, moving like a quiet storm with his finger steady on the trigger. Sweat covered his brow as he navigated the smoky corridors, passing Mesoamerican artifacts that were food for the inferno. Replicas of historic paintings were in flames, and he could feel the heat rising as he approached the sweltering stairwell. He glanced down over the fiery remains of the foyer, and spotted a lone wolf lingering by the monstrous tank: it was none other than Rico.

Ducking below the guardrail, Geronimo set the assault weapon atop the banister, then glared through the thermal

169

scope with one eye closed. Keeping a steady hand, he was surprised to see Rico aiming back at him with a grenade launcher. He cursed aloud as Rico squeezed the trigger, clambering away from the incoming cylinder. The spiraling bomb struck the bottom of the balcony, and he was hurled through a torrent of debris. The blast severed the floor supports, causing a portion of the upper deck to collapse, and he was pulled under the wreckage as he plummeted to the first level.

Rico proudly marched toward the fuming pile of destruction, passing mounds of dead bodies along the way. Although the damage was quite convincing, he was on a mission of retribution. Fully aware his employer was watching, he began digging through the rubble for confirmation, throwing aside immense fractured slabs of limestone with ease.

However, after lifting a shattered section of the gallery above his head, he was shocked to discover two active grenades buried among the fragments.

KABOOM!

Geronimo could feel the impact as he stumbled down an adjacent hallway. Lucky to be alive, he collapsed on the floor, tattered and bleeding from the head. Suffering from a concussion and a few broken bones, he could feel the flames on all sides, eating away remnants of the past in a gorge of ashes and embers. Suddenly, he heard the call of a wild beast, screaming for blood from the depths of hell. With wide eyes, he painfully staggered to his feet, then pointed his weapon toward the archway, expecting the devil himself. Astonishingly, a charbroiled Rico crashed through the granite like a wrecking ball, flanking his position. Rushing at full speed, he slammed into Geronimo with the strength of a freight train, spear tackling him through the adjacent wall. After barreling across the floor, Geronimo found himself sprawled flat on his back in the next chamber, fully immersed in a world of pain.

"Are you seeing this?" yelled Rico in a crazed manner.

Advancing with tenacity, he snatched Geronimo by the boots, then swung him through the air like a ragged doll. Geronimo flew across the room, then crashed through a giant display case, toppling over broken shards of glass as Rico continued to press forward.

"Can't you see I'm strong enough now?" he shouted. "Tell me I'm strong!"

He plucked Geronimo off the ground, then stamped him hard against another wall, cratering the surface. Submerged in agony, Geronimo managed to retract his knife, and stab Rico numerous times in the trapezius muscle, though it was virtually ineffective. Rico grabbed him by the wrist, and squeezed until the bones snapped within his grasp. Geronimo hollered out before catching a headbutt between the eyes, then Rico proceeded to tattoo his body with powerful hooks and uppercuts. Blinded by his own blood, Geronimo was pummeled deeper into the crater, until the wall eventually crumbled, and he landed amongst the rubble outside the museum.

Lying motionless across patches of dead grass, his enemy stood quietly at the threshold, casting a shadow over his body. Towering in the wind, Rico removed the blade protruding from his own flesh, then tossed it aside with total indifference. He turned back for the dusky foyer, hellbent on destroying any remaining Soldiers on his quest for godhood. However, after taking a few steps, he was stunned when Geronimo jumped him from behind.

"You hit like a bitch," he taunted, grappling Rico by the neck.

With the last of his strength, he quickly pressed his gun against Rico's helmet, then rapidly squeezed the trigger. Sparks blossomed in a colorful blaze before Rico tossed him away, somewhat impressed by his relentlessness. Geronimo tumbled through the air, then fell to the earth less than ten yards away, his frame bloody and broken.

Rico detached his damaged helmet, as if it were merely an inconvenience, then marched toward him with more persistence than death itself. "You must be a fool if you think you can kill me," he stated, void of emotion.

His body butchered and disfigured, Geronimo lay curled on the ground, squirming and coughing up blood. He felt like he had been hit by a bus and struck by lightning simultaneously. Nonetheless, he began laughing hysterically, mocking his assailant from the dirt, despite his own anguish.

Rico narrowed his eyes suspiciously, unaware that two active grenades were now glued to his lower back. "What the fuck are you laughing at?" he snapped.

BOOM!

In an instant, his molecules were scattered in a compressed explosion, painting the dreary field red with his organs. The force propelled Geronimo backward across the brown sward, sliding in a cloud of entrails. The blast echoed in the void, and once the dust settled, he was happily drenched in the remains of his enemy, laughing at death like a madman. A mangled mess, he was suffering from numerous major injuries, and every breath was torturous as he lay in the grass, staring at the sky in a stupor. Eventually, he could see the light of a new day piercing through the veil, and the soothing breeze gave him peace of mind as the world gradually became obsolete.

As the light slowly expanded, he was overcome by apparitions and lucid dreams. He saw past events and familiar faces, relived horrid mistakes and glorious triumphs. He thought about his mother, and the last time they ever spoke. He thought about his brother, and the bond they had, the laughs they shared. He thought about Kali; her touch, her smile, her spirit.

Suspended in limbo, a familiar voice pierced him through the static.

"Moe!" Kali yelled. She frantically ran to his side with Penny close behind, their eyes wide with shock. Fighting back the tears, she dropped to her knees and cradled him in her arms, silently praying for a miracle. "Oh my God," she sobbed.

"Kali?" he muddled. "…I was just about to call you."

"Don't talk, baby," she whimpered. "Let's just get out of here, okay?"

With the museum ablaze, Geronimo nodded deliriously as he welcomed her warm embrace, then uttered something incoherent before ultimately losing consciousness.

⊷════◉

After the darkest night, rays of light from the rising sun finally graced the peaks and valleys of Los Angeles. Like a page in a book, the sky slowly turned from deep purple to the golden promise of a new horizon. Birds were chirping, dogs were barking, and people across the city were preparing for the holiday weekend. It was officially Independence Day, a celebration of America's freedom from tyranny, and citizens were anxious to express their patriotism through an excess of alcohol, red meat, and fireworks.

On a secluded highway, Penny was driving north along the coast, destined for an isolated location far outside the city. Gulls were gliding over the expansive beach, while sunbeams reflected atop the crashing waves along the shoreline. Passing deserted high-risers sinking in dunes of sand, her mind was scattered in the ashes of the aftermath. The Soldiers were the only family she ever knew. Now, she belonged to a dynasty of ghosts, and their faces would haunt her forever. She could still see the flames; she could still smell the stench of burning flesh.

Red was slouched beside her, staring lethargically at the vast scenery, quietly contemplating their unknown future. With his fallen comrades on his heart, he wanted to cry; he wanted to scream; he wanted to explode. Instead, he sat in complete silence, pondering the truth, fixated on a harsh reality. As Victor's last words echoed in his psyche, his desire to fight increased exponentially. He decided to carry on, strengthen the resistance. He owed it to his brothers and sisters who sacrificed their lives. It was a debt he vowed to pay in blood ten-fold.

Kali was in the backseat, gazing out the window with vacant eyes. After so many tears, she was emotionally drained and physically exhausted, numb to the nightmare surrounding her. War was endless and brutal, soulless and unforgiving, with too many casualties to count. She was holding Geronimo in her arms, his body battered and broken. With his head in her lap, he eventually awoke to the sounds of the open road.

"Why's everybody so quiet?" he mumbled painfully.

His words were greeted by unanimous sighs of relief, as if everyone had been holding their breath. In that moment, the atmosphere was no longer that of despair, but of hope. As Penny reached back and gleefully squeezed his hand, Red expressed his solace with an easy grin, masking his exuberance.

"I knew he'd pull through," he said proudly. "He's too strong for them."

Kali simply looked down at Geronimo with joyful tears swelling in her eyes, then leaned over to kiss him in the light of a new day, a day she thought would never come.

CHAPTER FIFTEEN

Iron Hearts

In a small breakfast diner on Compton Avenue, Bunchy was sitting quietly at the bar, nursing a cup of Irish coffee in solitude. The meager restaurant housed a handful of customers, all seeking refuge and a hot meal. Surrounded by humble furnishings and autographed pictures of neighborhood celebrities, he was silently wrestling with new demons in the wake of a shattered existence. Alone in a cruel world, he was dealing with physical pain and crippling regret, struggling just to maintain.

"Hey, buddy," said a voice.

Stirred from his daze, he saw the manager standing behind the bar with a gentle smile. His sleeves were rolled up to his elbows, and a wet towel was draped over his shoulder.

"I'm not trying to get in your business," he said kindly. "But you're bleeding all over my counter."

Bunchy looked down at his hand crudely wrapped in bandages, then tucked it away beneath his coat, somewhat embarrassed.

"Can I get you anything else?" the manager asked. "Some napkins perhaps?"

Bunchy grinned politely, then casually finished his drink in one gulp. "More coffee," he grunted, pointing at the empty cup.

Still smiling, the manager retreated to fetch the pot from the kitchen. Passing an old television mounted on the wall, he quickly adjusted the volume before disappearing behind a silver door. On the thirty-two-inch screen, a program about the deadly nature of technology was cut short by the malicious undertones of an expensive advertisement:

"*Only on* 20 Minutes, *The Stay Ready Soldiers: how did a small group of would-be gangsters and thugs manage to terrorize an entire city? Was Tree Newman's message of violence truly a call for justice? Or was it simply a reflection of a homicidal maniac? Tomorrow night, we'll discuss the dangerous propaganda of the SRS, only on* 20 Minutes."

After the commercial, Bunchy almost choked on his coffee as a young woman shouted at the television.

"Are you fucking kidding me?" Dawn exclaimed, mouthful of pancakes. "What kind of shit is that?"

"Try yelling a bit louder," Anthony griped, holding a cold glass of water against his temple. "It makes my head feel a lot better."

The two teenagers were sitting in a tarnished booth by a large window, basking in the sun rays while nursing their wounds.

"Can you believe this shit?" she scowled, slamming her fist on the faded table.

"Why are you still yelling?" he mumbled. "I'm sitting right here."

"They're not thugs!" she argued. "They're the fucking good guys! They're superheroes!"

While patrons within earshot ignored her protests, Bunchy caught himself smiling as he focused on their conversation.

"Dawn, relax, nobody cares," said Anthony, playing with his scrambled eggs. "You're getting mad at the news for lying. That's like getting mad at the sharks for swimming."

"This shit's unbelievable," she groaned, trying to calm down. "It's just…I can't…I'm sorry. You're right. How're you feeling?"

"Peachy," he smirked. "It hurts to eat."

Eventually, the manager approached them as Dawn scraped the last of her plate clean. "Can I get you two anything else?" he asked politely.

"No thank you," Anthony declined. "Just bring us the bill, please."

"Oh, that's already been taken care of."

Anthony's expression was full of skepticism, while Dawn immediately stopped chewing with a similar uncertainty.

"Is this a joke?" she questioned, pointing her fork.

"Not at all," he answered. "In fact, you're welcome to whatever you want on the menu. Everything's already been paid for."

"In that case, I'll have a short-stack," Anthony smirked.

"Hold on," Dawn interjected. "Sorry, but I need to know who paid for this."

"Of course, it was that gentlemen over there…"

Pointing in Bunchy's direction, the manager was surprised to see an empty bar stool in his place. He shook his head with a wry grin, noticing the bountiful lump of cash beside a steaming cup of coffee. Without giving it another thought, he turned around to take their order, and Dawn hesitated before shrugging in compliance.

"Fuck it, give us all the short-stacks," she beamed.

Outside, Bunchy was bathing in the sun, looking past the pigeons and palm trees from a veteran's perspective. Raised in a different era, he was a descendent of gangsters and pimps, instilled with core principles and values that separated him from his peers. He was a product of his environment, which paradoxically made him a menace to society. Vilified his entire life, he was accustomed to being treated like a criminal; or a thug; or a terrorist. Thus, joining the Soldiers was an easy transition, not just for him, but for his cousin as well.

However, he never imagined them being referred to as superheroes, especially so adamantly. Limping to his car, he almost chuckled at the thought as he placed a cigarette between his lips.

Across the world, on an island in the Mediterranean Sea, Dr. Eugene Heidrich was sitting poolside at his luxury villa, nursing a glass of his most expensive wine in a plush fleece robe. Although he was well in his seventies, he had the appearance of a man in his early forties. Overlooking vast mountains and rolling hills, he was basking in a curtained cabana, casually watching two Russian bikini models swim topless by the infinity edge. Glowing lanterns were arranged about the travertine deck, and underwater lights made the pool change colors beneath a starlit sky. While enjoying the scenery, he was quietly contemplating his busy schedule for the upcoming week. His calendar was overloaded with meetings and lectures, lunches with liaisons and dinners with aristocrats, all to get investments for his latest scientific venture.

A centerfold rose from the water, and playfully tossed her G-string at him with a smile. "Why doesn't the good doctor join us?" she beckoned.

"Because he likes torturing us," splashed the other, pressing her wet breasts together.

He stood to his feet with a perverted grin, ready to disrobe.

"Excuse me, sir," said a voice. "I'm terribly sorry for disturbing you, but that American president keeps calling."

He turned around to see his personal butler standing nearby, holding fresh towels and a small mobile device. Breathing a sigh of annoyance, he reluctantly tightened his sash, then finished his glass with an ironic smirk. He calmly stepped to the ledge of the deck, and politely addressed his company. "Ladies, I must apologize," he announced. "But the sheep require salt. Feel free to keep each other warm."

After the women bouncily expressed their disapproval, he gave his butler a glance of dissent, then headed inside with the mobile device planted in his ear. His two-story villa was designed by an award-winning architect, featuring marble columns, floor-to-ceiling windows, and a contemporary décor. Passing unique sculptures and oil paintings, he walked upstairs to the seclusion of his home office, then gently closed the sliding doors behind him.

The room was a capsule of time, full of precious knowledge and priceless artifacts. Ancient weapons of war adorned the mahogany walls, and large bookshelves were cluttered with volumes of rare documents and precious manuscripts. There were photographs of himself posing with world leaders and people of influence, and a plethora of impressive awards celebrating his genius were on clear display. He poured a glass of bourbon at his minibar shaped like a globe, then sat atop the executive desk as he activated the device in his ear. "Well, someone's being persistent," he sighed.

"Is this line secure?"

"We wouldn't be talking if it weren't," Heidrich insisted. "Now, please make this quick. I'm entertaining a few guests tonight, and it'd be rude of me to keep them waiting."

"Okay, I'll be brief. Listen, I know what we agreed to, but this is too much. I got congress literally up my ass, watching every fucking move I make. They want to subpoena my entire administration! Democrats hate me, republicans hate me, the media hates me...I think the First Lady's having an affair with my lawyer, and now, there's this thing in LA. Mayor Dernum's whining and crying in my ear, saying he's got dead bodies all over the fucking city! Look, I realize you and your associates have your own agenda, but this shit's getting out of control!"

"Mr. President," Heidrich interrupted. "Does this little rant of yours have a point?"

"Yeah! At this rate, I'll get impeached before Christmas!"

"I see," Heidrich nodded, pacing in front of his desk. "Must I remind you; my associates and I are the ones who got you elected in the first place. You had ambitions of fame, and title, and power. And we generously gave it to you."

"But I never wanted it to be like this!"

"Please, don't be so naive. We're ushering in the next phase of humanity. Do you understand what that means? That means weeding out the herd. Certain steps must be taken; certain standards must be met."

"I don't know…there has to be another way…"

"You can't stop the future, Mr. President. And I shouldn't have to tell you what happens to those who try. But, since we're being so candid, allow me to share this with you. Success is based on attitude, and attitude is based on perspective. Where you see chaos, I see opportunity. I see a man fighting to keep the citizens safe from domestic terrorism. I see the resurgence of patriotism, the reestablishment of traditional American values: life, liberty, justice. And with the proper spin, I see a strong campaign for reelection."

The line fell silent as he sipped his bourbon, calmly waiting for a response.

"You really think so?" he heard eventually.

"Absolutely," Heidrich smiled. "When people are scared, they'll believe anything."

"Yeah, you're right…I can spin this…presidents spin shit all the time. I'll just say what you said: I'm fighting domestic terrorism; I'm fighting to protect the people! Hell, I'm the only one trying to keep this country together!"

"Everything that's going on only proves that the people need you," Heidrich coaxed. "They need a leader like you. Someone strong, someone fearless, someone willing to make the hard decisions without thinking."

"That's me! That's what I'm all about!"

"Then stick to the script. We're trusting you to keep the people in line. If you're unable to do so, then we'll find someone who can."

"No-no, I can do this! Just, uh…I'll figure something out."

"Good to know," Heidrich grinned. "Now, try not to worry. I'm taking a trip to DC in a few days; we'll talk then. Good day, Mr. President."

"Uh, yeah…good day to you too. I mean goodnight, have a good night…"

Removing the gadget from his ear, Heidrich ended the call with a subtle look of annoyance. Finishing his drink, he returned to the minibar for a refill, then walked across the room to one of the many bookcases. Gently swirling the liquor in his glass, he activated a hidden switch behind the face frame, and the entire wall unit pivoted open, revealing a secret room with a multi-monitor workstation. He typed a sequence of numbers on one of the keypads, and footage from the Black Hawks' assault began playing on every screen. As he studied the sensitive material in silence, his butler entered the office with a silver dish of premium cigars.

"I'm truly sorry about Rico, sir," he said. "He was… special."

"He was expensive," Heidrich uttered, selecting a cigar for himself. "He had too much pride, too much ego. It clouded his judgment in the end."

He paused the playback of Rico's feed, then typed a set of commands that expanded and sharpened the image, revealing a perfectly clear picture of Geronimo's face. He lit the cigar as he stared intently at the screen, intrigued by the mystery man who destroyed his billion-dollar weapon singlehandedly.

"And what of this gentleman here?" his butler asked. "A new specimen?"

"Well, he's definitely on my radar…"

ABOUT THE AUTHOR

Not much is known about Michael West. According to legend, he comes from a land by the sea, a place at the end of the sun, and only appears when he has a story to tell. Many believe he's an old soul from a forgotten time, a lost culture, decimated in the conquest of history. Others claim he is merely a symbol, a product of the people, reflecting the dreams and atrocities of a fragile society. Whether he's more than a man, or simply a myth, only one thing's for certain: not much is known about Michael West.